"Yo, Forest."

"Yes, this is For...hey, Tony!"

"Forest, do you know if O'Brien was right-handed or left-handed? Or was he, what do you call it? Either one."

"Ambidextrous."

"I never remember the word. It sounds dirty."

"Let me think. He was...wait a minute...he was right-handed. Yeah, I'm sure of it. Right-handed."

"Do me a favor, will you, man?"

"Sure."

"Pretend you have a pistol—a thirty-eight special—in your right hand. Just pretend."

"Okay, though I haven't the slightest idea what a thirty-eight special looks like."

"No sweat. Just pretend it's a capgun. You holding it? In your right hand?"

"Yeah."

"Bring the weapon up to shoot yourself in your temple."

Forest does as directed.

"Now which temple—left or right—is your weapon aimed at?"

"My right temple."

"Now, keeping the weapon in your right hand try to shoot yourself in your left temple."

Impossible. If you were right-handed and wanted to shoot yourself you'd put the gun to your right temple.

"Did the papers say where he shot himself, Forest?"

"Yes. In the left temple. Tony?"

ALSO BY CHESTER AARON

Whispers
Garlic Kisses and Tasty Hugs
Willa's Poppy
Gideon

MURDER BY METAPHOR

CHESTER AARON

ZUMAYA ENIGMA   2009   AUSTIN TX

MURDER BY METAPHOR
© 2009 by Chester Aaron
ISBN 978-1-934841-52-5

Cover art and design © Gary Trow

"Zumaya Enigma" and the raven colophon are trademarks of Zumaya Publications LLC, Austin TX.

Look for us online at
http://www.zumayapublications.com

Library of Congress Cataloging-in-Publication Data

Aaron, Chester.
 Murder by metaphor / Chester Aaron.
   p. cm.
 ISBN 978-1-934841-52-5 (alk. paper) ~ ISBN 978-1-934841-53-2 (electronic)
   1.   College teachers~Fiction. 2.   Poets~Crimes against~Fiction. 3.   Police~California~San Francisco~Fiction. 4.   San Francisco (Calif.)~Fiction. I. Title.
 PS3551.A57M87 2009
 813'.54~dc22
                                    2009029896

To Miriam Block and Andrea Young and Thomas Farber. All three are living proof that friendship and love are facts, not themes for poets to exploit. Thanks, Miriam, thanks, Andrea, thanks, Tom.

For each ecstatic instant
We must an anguish pay
In keen and quivering ration
To the ecstasy.

For each beloved hour
Sharp pittances of years—
Bitter contested farthings—
And Coffers heaped with Tears!

— Emily Dickinson

CHAPTER 1

To leave space in the garage for Emerald's new blue Mazda RX-7, Forest Butler parks his red ten-year-old Toyota Corolla at the curb. Forest, as he takes several deep breaths to build energy for the dash through the rain, considers the newspapers, books and brief-case beside him on the passenger seat and, on the back seat, the canvas overnight bag. Books, briefcase, newspapers must be carried inside. The overnight bag, which contains the clothes he used in Missouri over the weekend, can remain in the car. Emerald can throw the clothes into the laundry tomorrow or the next day.

Now! Go, Forest. Now!

With briefcase clasped in his left hand, this morning's *New York Times* and *Wall Street Journal* (both read on the plane) and four books held pre-cariously between left arm and body, Forest exhales, waits, takes another deep breath, opens the car door, steps outside. While thumb and forefinger of his right hand fight and finally conquer the car's interior locking device the heavy briefcase dangles from the last three fingers of his left hand. Managing to escape

1

the snare of the oleander bushes at the curb and, not daring to sprint for fear the books and newspapers will tumble into a puddle, Forest scuttles like a crippled crab as far as the redwood fence, where, with a well-practiced bump of hip and thrust of shoulder, he knocks open the gate.

After leaning back against it until he hears the latch click, Forest arranges books and newspapers more securely under his left arm for the final dash for the porch.

Hunched over, keyring caught and held now between thumb and forefinger of his right hand (briefcase dangling), he makes his way along the alternating curves of the brick path, successfully avoiding the deepest puddles until, just inches from the first of five steps leading up to the porch, water laps over the top of his right shoe and soaks the entire foot. On the porch, in the shelter of the overhang (books and newspapers slipping slowly from beneath his left arm), Forest, on the first try, unlocks and opens the front door as he kicks the plastic-bagged *San Francisco Chronicle* from porch to interior.

Inside, leaving the door open behind him, he rushes through the living room. He reaches the clawfooted oak dining table just in time for newspapers and books to drop to the top and continue, falling onto the Beluchistan carpet.

On his return to close the front door he curses the wet sock that has slid down past his right heel to settle like a boiled potato beneath the arch of his foot. Back at the table and standing over the furnace-vent in the oak floor, he unties the laces of his shoe and removes the sock. Heat drifts up through the vent to and through foot to knee to thigh, as Forest slips the *Chronicle* free of its plastic bag.

NOTED POET SUICIDE

IN SAN FRANCISCO

2

He staggers back, as if some intruder, darting from behind the window curtain, has punched five blows into his body midway between belt and chin. The caption beneath the photograph: Award-winning Poet Dead at 46. First sentence, lede paragraph: *Famed San Francisco poet Farleigh O'Brien was found dead this morning in his Telegraph Hill apartment in San Francisco.*

Second sentence, still the lede paragraph: *According to police, O'Brien died of what appeared to be a self-inflicted gunshot wound to the left temple.*

Forest knows the source of the front-page photograph. It had been lifted from the jacket flap of Farleigh O'Brien's latest book, *Riding the Wing of the Condor.* There is O'Brien, sitting on the deck of his High Sierra cabin, wearing a pair of those pre-faded and pre-scuffed jeans designed to pass for range-scarred cowboy attire. Tilted back on his head: what O'Brien had called "my seven-gallon Stetson," a battered black hat he had bought ten or twelve years ago in Austin, Texas, where, on the basis of the success of his first collection of poems, he'd been invited to read. The first step in what was to be a very rapid climb to national and almost immediate international fame.

O'Brien's feet cannot be seen in the photograph, but Forest knows they are encased in cowboy boots which, their warranty promised, would smell of sweat and horse dung for a year after purchase. A free plastic bag of lotion had accompanied the boots, recommended for application in a year to restore the aroma for an additional year.

Forest checks his watch as he limps to the phone. It is five-thirty. Paul Scarborough has left the campus and is at this moment racing along Coyote Road on his way home for the first of three—or four or five—pre-dinner martinis.

Self-inflicted gunshot wound...

3

Not just a gunshot wound but a *self-inflicted* gunshot wound.

In the temple. The temple, for Chrissake!

Temple: residence of the mind.

Mind: the temple of the human soul.

Forest hears again Paul Scarborough's "That man, and I use the term loosely, has point-five-degree mind and zero soul."

Just six months ago, in the *New York Review of Books*, in a four-page evaluation of the current state of American poetry, the famed (unjustly so, in the views of both Forest Butler and Paul Scarborough) critic Ian Christopher had baptized Farleigh O'Brien "The holy font of contemporary American culture, our own Homer of our own wine-dark seas." Within days San Francisco's *California Literary Review* (the West Coast's shadow of the NYRB) fell into the lengthening line of sycophants. "One of the finest critical and creative minds and spirits since the grand and elegant days of Eliot, Pound, Wilson, Burke..."

How soon we forget. Or, if we are sycophants, how little we want to know.

Sandy Messer, editor of *California Literary Review*, is thirty-six. Her memory (the source of her own stories and poems) goes back no farther than her own fascination with her own flatulent escape from her own mother's womb. Pound, that demented fascist, grand? Let alone elegant?

And Pound's patron saint Count Ciano Mussolini—also grand? Also elegant? Ciano, the son of *il Duce*, had bombed stone-age natives in Abyssinia and later described the explosions as "blooming flowers." Ciano Mussolini—elegant?

The publisher of O'Brien's *Riding the Wings of the Condor* is Holy Mountain Press, which had announced just six months ago that it would be presenting Farleigh O'Brien's collected works in a limited three-volume leather-bound autographed edition. Setting up poet and publisher for a second Pulitzer and, eventually (should the hype succeed) a Nobel, which would rescue both poet and publisher from financial—Paul Scarborough: "But not moral"—bankruptcy.

Paul, relying on what he referred to as "my aboveground network," had informed Forest that O'Brien was a sheltered (meaning secret) stockholder and board member of Holy Mountain Press.

"I can't believe that, Paul. Is that true?"

"Forest, I'm pained in the—what does Goldstein call it? Kishke. I'm pained in my kishke at your suspicious nature. Have I ever lied to you? Well, have I ever lied to you more than twice in the same conversation? Have I lied to you recently?"

One thing is certain: regardless of motive, there will be no more sailing across our own wine-dark seas for our own American Homer. All that is left of that famed critical mind and poetic spirit, as well as its temple, must still, this evening, lie splattered on the walls of whichever room of O'Brien's Telegraph Hill apartment had been host to his suicide.

"Gross," his students would moan.

"Disgusting," Emerald would say. "Absorutry disgusting, Forest."

Forest checks his watch. Where is Emerald? It is 6:25. Heavy traffic on the Bay Bridge?

Back to the *Chronicle* photograph of Farleigh O'Brien, back to that face of an aging fraternity pledge, to the knit sweater draped about the shoulders, sleeves loosely knotted at the neck, strong white teeth that prove the existence of childhood diets of orange juice and milk and fluoride toothpaste, raffish seven-gallon black Stetson. All of it, Farleigh had hoped at the time of the photo-shoot, all of it suggesting the secret inner soul of a thorny-hearted, tight-muscled Texas Ranger.

In your dreams, Farleigh.

5

Forest, a bit pained by his mindless selection of imagery, grunts. *Fraternity pledge* had come too quickly, too easily. As did—does—*Texas Ranger*. Well, let's see. What might ring true about Farleigh O'Brien?

This: Precociously portly, middle-aged, recently unearthed fossil of a flower-child, long hair elaborately cut and professionally shaped beneath the ever-present Stetson to conceal the growing spread of glossy skull. It is the flower-child choirboy frat-pledge charm, enhanced by that carefully honed demeanor of angelic innocence that is—had been—as much a part of O'Brien's persona as his (admit it, Forest!) excellent mind.

Admitted. Paul Scarborough's off-stage voice: *Shame on you, Forest.*

Actually, Paul, a mind beyond excellence. I'd call it brilliant.

Paul Scarborough: *Okay. Compromise. Let's stop at excellent.*

Wrong, Paul. Brilliant!

Paul, at that now-remembered exchange, had held both nostrils with thumb and forefinger of one hand and cleared the air with a wave of his other hand.

"The man simply remembers every word of every book he's ever read and every lecture he's ever heard, and like a trained Labrador, he retrieves, whenever necessary, the appropriate phrases to please. Tail wagging, panting, he lays them at the feet of *Fresh Air*'s Terry Gross and Michiko Kakutani and they swoon. Brilliant mind, no. Brilliant autodidact, yes. Hypnotist, you betcha."

"Your language is the language of a poet, Professor Scarborough."

"That foul foul word again! Wash your mouth, Forest. Here's a gin-and-tonic."

Paul will be home in five minutes. He will require at least two martinis before he can talk shop, meaning talk campus gossip. And gossip there will be. More lamentation than gossip.

Give him an hour. Forest checks his watch. Emmy will be home by then, so he will need to be more restrained, more guarded. But he must talk to Paul soon.

Back to the *Chronicle*, to the front page, to the photograph in which Farleigh is wearing, under the knotted sweater, one of those safari shirts intentionally bruised in production to suggest treks through thorny brush and charges by angry rhinos. The shirt and other such pieces of Hemingwayesque clothing can be purchased at Banana Republic. O'Brien, like several other men (and only men) in San Francisco, earns free safari clothes by condoning use of name and photo for Banana Republic's mail-order catalogue. Like the directors of the board of Banana Republic, like his catalogue colleagues, O'Brien has never been closer to Africa than a well-publicized signature on a petition to free Nelson Mandela.

"So the bastard's dead."

Forest glances over his shoulder to locate that intruder who, after having punched him five times, has just spoken those four words aloud. But he is alone in the house.

"Killed himself." His own voice again.

As much as O'Brien had disgusted him, had frustrated and angered him, he had never wished the poor bugger dead. Sick, sure. Perhaps very sick. A disabling illness for ten or fifteen years, perhaps. Sick enough to be frightened of what he sees in his own heart and mind and recovering, possibly, to repent.

But dead? At forty-six?

"Suicide."

7

No. Forest, in his wildest moments of scorn for O'Brien, would never have thought the man capable of suicide. Certainly never capable of using a gun.

Sleeping pills, maybe. Or, like three other poets of recent memory, a leap from the Golden Gate Bridge. Most likely: in a tightly insulated garage on a rainy night, a hose from the exhaust of his car into the front seat, windows closed. Now cracks a noble heart. *Good night, sweet prince* (murmured to himself as he struggles toward final inhalation?) *and flights of angels sing thee to thy rest!*

Forest pauses to concentrate on the montage of colliding images: O'Brien in his room, in his apartment on Telegraph Hill; O'Brien pointing the gun at his temple; O'Brien's finger pulling against the trigger.

He almost shouts, "Stop!" The sense of a life lost, even the life of Farleigh O'Brien, brings tears of real remorse to Forest's eyes, and he finds it difficult to admit that he ever participated in malevolent thoughts or deeds regarding Farleigh O'Brien. He has certainly never hated the man. Good Lord, when has he hated anyone? Nixon? Kissinger? Reagan? Bush? He'd not even hated *them*, he'd simply convicted them all, in his own mind, as war criminals.

Farleigh was certainly not in their league. He, well...

Farleigh O'Brien was simply the ultimate politician of aesthetics.

O'Brien, preparing for his eight o'clock class, must have decided he'd had enough. But enough of what? And that weapon. Where the hell could O'Brien have gotten a gun? A shotgun, as required by Hemingway? Or had Big Ernie used a rifle? A pistol or a revolver? And what's the difference between a pistol and a revolver?

Impossible to imagine Farleigh O'Brien—the pacifist, the humanist, one of those meek who shall inherit the earth—bartering in a sleazy pawn shop for a lethal weapon or prowling the streets of Oakland, whispering, dealing. A legitimized peacenik so filled with anti-violence it became a daily, hourly diet. Remember Vietnam? Yes, Remember Vietnam!

In the early days of the Vietnam War, when he'd faced the threat of being drafted, O'Brien had been deferred on the basis of his conscientious objection to killing man or beast. That conscience prevailed still as recently as a year ago—more than twenty years after the Vietnam war ended—at the publication dinner of his *Deer, Bear and Blue Lupine*, a collection of poems celebrating the mythic unconscious. O'Brien had catalogued what can only be described as primitive joys (quote-unquote) experienced during a weekend in the Delta shooting ducks and a second weekend in the high Sierras shooting elk. And, with three bearded and rifle-toting backwoodsmen always shielding him at the trap lines, three days in the Arctic trapping the ferocious wolverine.

And that night at Chez Panisse!

To celebrate the announcement of his having won the De Pesta Medal for his first volume of poems and essays (dinner at Chez Panisse in Berkeley), O'Brien, wearing his Stetson and his scented cowboy boots, had presented the chef with sixteen steaks cut from the haunches of the elk he had shot. After dinner, over brandy, submitting to persistent requests, he'd read, in almost mournful humility, the final poem ("The Ochered Buck") in the collection.

The Ochered Buck

on the sandstone wall
stumbles falls my own buck
heart leaps my scrotum fills
I the slope-headed painter
in the cave

eat the heart of my kill
with bloody fingers

"I always," O'Brien had written on the title page of the copy purchased by Emerald, "precede each shot with a Zen prayer: May your soul rest forever in the *shikiyu* of your ancestors who never die."

(Footnote: shikiyu: a burial site on a hill that overlooks the sea.)

Paul, on the way home (Emerald and Maria Scarborough in the back seat): "Another puerile fantasy of a meek and mild Boy Scout attaining karmic machismo. What our friend and dear colleague Professor Goldstein calls *vershtunkena* bullshit. Or should it be *vershtunkene*? Does Yiddish have gender rules, Forest? Is bullshit masculine or feminine? Masculine, obviously. But singular or plural? It's a collective noun so it has to be singular."

Within one week of the publication of *Deer, Bear and Blue Lupine* critics and editors and other poets, as well as Foundations all over the nation had, like hungry kittens, dashed to lap up O'Brien's whipped-cream Zen. To this day, only three of the perhaps one hundred literary foundations in the United States had failed to sanctify the man.

Forest's six-month sabbatical has kept him away from the campus for the last three months so now, home from Missouri, he almost regrets not being on campus today when the proverbial shit must have hit the proverbial fan. Members of the English Department have probably wrapped Saturn Hall in black crepe. The intellectual skin-heads (Paul's nomenclature) throughout the Bay Area are surely, as Forest reads, mounting the first wave of what is certain to be a tide of orgiastic obituaries.

Up the stairs from the basement garage come footsteps.

Emerald is home! My beloved Emerald!

10

Here is Emerald Hyashi Butler, home from the wars. She runs up the interior steps and unlocks the door that opens into the kitchen. After stomping the water from her boots onto the heavy mat placed inside the kitchen door that morning, she removes and shakes the plastic bonnet that protects her thick black hair. While freeing herself of her raincoat: "Forest, your feet soaked. You raincoat drip on rug!"

Forest looks up. He apologizes with a pout and head-bow, as if the rug is hers alone.

"Carpet," he says. "Beluchistan carpet. Four thousand-five-hundred-sixty dollars and seventeen cents."

As he permits Emerald to tug one and then the other arm of his coat he shifts the *Chronicle* to each hand as that hand becomes available.

"You heard?" He shows holds out the front page.

Emerald, ignoring the paper, carries their coats into the bathroom.

"I read the story," she says, on her return. "And radio. I'rl (the slightest difficulty with the L, indicating a preliminary stage of distraction or anger or, worse, distress.) get your slippers." Back with his slippers, bending to fit each foot inside the fleece: "My God, you worse than my father, and he's armost ninety. News on every station. Terrible." Risk after risk with the L. "He so young, so wise."

"And so dead. We must refer to him from now on in the past tense."

"We call Aprirl perhaps?"

"Why? They've been divorced for five years."

"Four. She still loves him." *Roves him.*

"Loved," Forest advises her.

"She'rl be..." and Emerald, impatient, waits for assistance.

"Destroyed?"

She shakes her head.

"Delighted?"

11

She stomps her foot. "Must not make fun."

"Devastated?"

"Yes. Devastated, You would know before you pick up the paper if you pray your radio in your car. You not hear news from the airport?" Reversion to her transitory but historic problems with the language seems now to bring her close to tears.

"Radio. *Il Barbiere di Seville*. Pavarotti. First things first, my beloved."

Emerald rolls her eyes. "No news report on prane?"

"Emerald, this is not Japan. The death of a famous poet, much less an infamous poet, is hardly competition for Bush heroics or the antics of Ahmedinejad or the triple bypass of the Communist Party's heart. That stuff is news, Emerald. I didn't even buy a set of earphones. I'd have had to plow through six rock stations to find one news station. I wonder who'll take over his classes. Mary Beth, perhaps, if she recovers."

"Mishima's death on the front pages aw over Japan."

"Mishima, my dear, was a presence. O'Brien is a past."

"Forest, I am upset. We go out for supper. I feel rike I did when Kennedy died."

"Kennedy was assassinated, Emerald."

She gasps, looking for a moment as if the sobs in her throat might pop free through her closed lips. "I want to be with friends tonight."

"I'm not a friend, my beloved?"

"Maria. We call Scarboroughs. Maria is...what? Devastated. The Scarboroughs prob'ry hoping we carl."

Two barely passing grades. Forest knows her facility with the language will return as she begins to relax. At ease, she will again sound as American as most of his colleagues, certainly more than most of his students. "Good idea. I'd like to talk to Paul. It is strange, isn't it? Suicide. Who'd have thought he'd ever find the guts for that. Or the brains. Well, he doesn't—"

"Don't say. That disgusting. Why you have to be so...so...?"

Without looking up from the newspaper: "Disgusting?"

Emerald stomps her foot again.

"Wry?" he tries, still reading. "Which reminds me. I'll have a drink."

She glares, refusing to do his suggested bidding. Defying him to request again so she might refuse again?

"No, no," he says. "Let me. I'll get it. Would you like one, dear? Cynical?"

"Why you be so cynicarl? Yes, I want drink. Bourbon."

"You only drink bourbon on our anniversary. On ice?"

"Yes. We have soda. Soda, too. I don't think anyone predict who commit suicide. And suicide is not...what? Humiriating?"

"Not in Japan, perhaps. And not for your warrior-hero, Mishima. Americans however do not—"

"I'm going carl Scarboroughs. And prease, we have dinner, you and Paw not be evirl. The man is dead."

"Paul? Dead? No one told me."

"Can't you forgive Farreigh his rittew...?"

"Conspiracies?"

"Forest!"

"Eccentricities?"

Emerald, receiver to her ear, hand over her eyes, speaks hushed but explosive Japanese into the mouthpiece.

"Peccadiloes?"

No telling what the aggrieved Emerald would have done had Maria not answered the telephone.

Forest takes advantage of the moment to prepare his gin-and-tonic and Emerald's bourbon-and-soda, which he takes to her as the two women exchange moans of remorse and words of reassurance. In the living-room with his drink, he checks his watch. Five minutes before six.

He rereads the story, searching for facts he might have missed. Such as the lead paragraph's second sentence: "*According to police, O'Brien died of what appeared to be a self-inflicted gunshot wound to the left temple.*"

...appeared to be...self-inflicted...

Self-inflicted.

Appeared to be.

So, it might not be suicide. Jesus H. Christ! Someone might have murdered Farleigh O'Brien!

Who could have...would have...?

Is there one professor besides Professors Forest Butler and Paul Scarborough who has even snickered at O'Brien's creative and intellectual theatrics? Not one. With the exception of Mary Beth, the other twelve members of the Department have permanently puckered lips and calloused knees from kneeling to kiss O'Brien's ass.

Forest turns on the television set at six o'clock, finds a local news program and, after a long sip from his glass, sits back into the pillows, facing the screen. He stretches his right foot toward the flameless fireplace. Patrice Fernandez alerts her viewers to the fact that after the next commercial break there will be a report on the suicide of San Francisco's prize-winning poet, Farleigh O'Brien.

Emerald completes her phone call in time to arrive at the sofa when the report begins and to stand behind her husband. With each new fact presented by Fernandez she murmurs, "Oh no, oh no."

When the screen, with Fernandez's voice-over, is filled with a new and different photograph, it is Forest's turn to gasp. This photo was taken four years ago at the Sikorski's pool, the day O'Brien won the Pulitzer. On the following day, Farleigh had appeared on campus wearing his Stetson and boots.

Emerald's sobs, behind Forest's back, are dainty little hiccups. He leans forward, squinting. He fumbles hastily in his breast pocket for his glasses and, not finding them there, drops to his knees and crawls close to the screen, squinting more intently.

"That photograph's been altered," he says. "He had a bald spot in the original. Remember? I took that photo. He was in the pool. I was standing on the diving board, shooting down. His bald spot gleamed in the sunlight. He hated the photo when he saw it. Remember? No one has seen that bald spot since that day. He hides it under that damn sombrero."

"Stetson. He carl it Stetson."

"Emmy, that photo has been retouched. His hair looks thicker than yours." Forest, with a sigh, sits back on his haunches. "Farleigh, you vain asshole."

Emerald rushes into the bathroom.

After the news program ends, Forest turns off the set, makes himself a second gin-and-tonic, drops once again onto the sofa. He leans forward over *The Chronicle* spread open on the floor. Continued on display: the headline, the photograph, the story. NOTED POET SUICIDE IN SAN FRANCISCO

He picks up the paper, folding it until only the photo is visible. *You sorry son-of-a-bitch, Farleigh. You paid someone to retouch that photo. Where the hell did all that silly vanity get you? A bullet through your bald head. Vain, delusional, petty, right up to the end.*

Vain, vain, go away, little Farleigh wants to play...

A sudden twinge of pain in the cavity containing his heart. Where has that pain come from? Could it be remorse? Could it be a warning from God of his own (not God's but his, Forest's) mortality? Behind him, Emerald, slamming drawers and doors, moves

15

down the hall from the bedroom to the bathroom. He hears water rushing into the tub. *O'Brien, you're on the wings of your condor now. You looking down or up?*

In his study, at his desk, speaking low even though there is no chance of Emerald overhearing, Forest calls Information and asks for the number of the San Francisco Police Department.

"Homicide, please. Hello, I'm trying to contact Sergeant Tony Coniglio. I was one of Tony's professors at Saint Catherine's College."

On the second transfer, a man identifies himself as Sergeant Leroy McCafferty.

"Sergeant, I'm trying to locate—"

"Yeah. Detective Coniglio. He's out...No, here he is. Hey, Tony, one of your old professors at Saint Catherine's. You flunked your final exam."

Laughter and jeers in the background.

"This is Detective Coniglio."

"Tony, Forest Butler here."

"Yo, Forest. How the hell are you, man? I've been thinking about you. This suicide. O'Brien."

"That's what I called about. So, it *is* suicide? Is that official?"

Voice low, conspirator to colleague: "Where are you? You gonna be home tonight? Around ten o'clock?"

"I'll make it a point to be."

Voice still low: "Call you around ten." Louder: "How's Emerald?"

"She's fine, Tony."

"Hey, man, I want an invitation to dinner. I've been over here in the city for ten years, and I haven't had one Japanese meal to even come near the food Emerald makes."

"You got it. I'll talk to her tonight, and we'll set a date."

Forest continues staring at the phone after he returns it to its cradle, as if, in response to the correct code, a collection of secrets stored in that cradle will be divulged.

CHAPTER 2

In his study, unpacking his briefcase, Professor Forest Butler, the persistent master of research, knows he exaggerates his interest in the contents only to distract himself from immediate questions about immediate concerns. He does pause to ask himself why the word *crime* pops into his mind at this moment, and why the word *suicide* follows the word *crime* and the word *killer* follows *suicide* and...

But what the hell does all this intellectual masturbation have to do with Farleigh O'Brien? Is he, unwilling to deal with the death of Farleigh O'Brien, trying to distract himself from Emerald's troubling behavior the past few weeks?

Make that months, Forest. And not Farleigh's death, Forest. Make that Farleigh's suicide.

After all, hasn't Tony Coniglio—Detective Tony Coniglio—verified the probability of suicide? Was it probability...or possibility?

Is that—Farleigh's suicide—what has disturbed Emerald this evening?

If so, why?

Why should the death of Farleigh O'Brien, by suicide or homicide, have such an impact on Emerald? Is it O'Brien's suicide, or could it be her mother in distant Japan? Could her mother be sick again? That liver cancer diagnosed two years ago—has Emerald received a letter indicating...?

Is Emerald protecting him, her beloved Forest, from her own anguish?

Is his beloved Emerald...?

Emerald Hyashi Butler—still, after twenty years of marriage, the inscrutable Oriental. A woman who had always—even in Japan—been too easily persuaded that she should share the woes of those less fortunate. Think Hibakushka, the Hiroshima victims. She, Emerald Hyashi, a Joan of Arc-san—born in Kyoto ten years after the war ended. Kyoto, that city of purple hills and crystal streams. She, Emerald Hyashi, has designated herself their savior. She, Emerald Hyashi, with the whispery voice of a submissive child and the timid baby-step walk and serene angelic smile.

She—*Japanese woman hopes to meet.* She, Emerald Hyashi, the American male's version (at least this American male's version) of the legendary Japanese wife offering herself in that ubiquitous Personals world finally and not too reluctantly examined by Professor Forest Butler. She, Emerald Hyashi.

Forest Butler had convinced himself after the second letter (almost two years before he met her), that she, this servant-mistress-wife-mother, Emerald Hyashi Butler, was the only woman he could be devoted to, the only woman with whom he, Forest Butler, dared consider sharing his life. Meaning, it turned out, the only woman he could love. And love her he did. And does.

An example of Emerald Hyashi's Oriental inscrutability: within six months of their marriage she had on her own book shelf in her own room every book (in Japanese, of course) Yukio Mishima had ever

20

written while—delicately but persistently, and always without hostility—ignoring Forest's efforts to solicit her impressions of Mishima's words. As if, given his heritage and his professorial aura, Forest Butler would never be able to comprehend that great man's significance.

When the film *Mishima* arrived at the Elmwood Theater six years ago Emerald had gone alone four times, and had so persistently shrugged off Forest's questions that he finally gave up asking them. About both books and film.

After all, has he ever discussed his gods, Twain and Faulkner, with her?

Never. But at least he had read Mishima. She had only *tried* to read Faulkner. He had offered her Faulkner's *The Old Man*. His own copy, a prized first edition. When she finally (after eight days? ten?) confessed that the opening sentence—the antithesis of the spare, precise Japanese aesthetic—had overwhelmed her, Professor Butler had demonstrated the compassion and tact that had earned him tenure and respect in academia.

"Try Huck Finn, darling. It's the spine of the body of American culture."

His suggestion was followed by a stare, those big black eyes bulging. Why wouldn't a brief American metaphor be understood by someone whose language thrives on the haiku, a national glorification of metaphor?

"A book a spine of the body?"

"Indulge me, my beloved. Just try."

After four attempts (a page and a half each time) she'd set Huck Finn aside, and Forest never again mentioned either Twain or Faulkner.

She returned to the reading and rereading of each of the seven Mishima books stored on the small shelf above her desk in the corner of their bedroom.

"Our bedroom," she had written her parents, "is as large as Tofukuji temple in Kyoto." Emerald, from

21

that desk in that bedroom as large as the Tofukuji Temple, could gaze down onto very narrow Tammalpais Avenue and, when she chose not to park in the single-car garage, could distinguish her sky-blue Mazda RX-7 from neighbors' cars at the curb. "Our house number is seven-seven-seven. Good fortune forever for me here, mama-san."

Forest had been moderately shocked at her purchase of that Mazda a year ago.

"You bought an RX-seven? My God, my dear, it's so...so expensive."

"I earn a high salary, Forest. Anyway, it is used. Two years old. Not so expensive."

Sary. And *Owed.*

"Did you have a choice of color?"

"Yes. Blue."

Brue.

Why the tension that affected her struggle with letters and syllables when under high stress?

"Well, I must say, blue's your color."

"So okay with you? I'm not bad woman to buy such expensive car?"

"My incandescent love, it's impossible for Emerald Hyashi to be a bad woman."

She danced across the room to the antique stand, where she wrestled with the huge Merriam-Webster dictionary. "How do speew in-can...in-can-what?"

"I..."

"Wait, wait. Okay. Speew. I..."

"...c-a-n..."

"Wait, wait." She laughed as she followed his carefully laid trail of letters.

The sound of Emerald's laughter, when Emerald Hyashi Butler is happy, contains, Forest once mused aloud to Paul Scarborough, what has to be memories of temple bells. That would have to be the bells of Tofukuji, one of the Five Great Temples of Kyoto. Always-calm Emerald, always-serene Emerald—like

22

the great temples, like the scented gardens, the floral canals, the raked gardens.

But there are moments.

Moments when, distraught, brooding about her aged parents, Emerald Hyashi Butler is possibly like a Kyoto autumn, her favorite season—hesitant, reticent, moody.

While visiting her parents four autumns ago Emerald sent Forest a letter. Practiced, complacent, assured, at peace, she had not had the slightest need for the dog-eared Japanese-English dictionary or for what she called, "My personoh friend"—the *Strunk & White Handbook of Style*, wrapped in rose-petal paper purchased in Kyoto and then wrapped again in elaborately taped plastic wrap for added protection against smudge and moisture.

Forest keeps this letter in the lacquered box she brought him from her first visit to Kyoto, along with every letter she has written him during her three subsequent visits to reassure her parents that here in America she is continuing happy, healthy and wise.

> I see Kyoto again lying silent inside mist. Streets are wet, shiny, hills are green green. Tangerine trees are in bloom. Monks ride by, they peddle their bicycles so slowly, cowls of their robes over their heads.
>
> Yesterday I wished so much you did not teach, you could come to Kyoto with me. At the Heian Shrine, in every spot of sunlight, I watched my face dance in every small pool of water. How you would have said Oh and Ah at many beautiful girls meditating at edges of ponds. Every gate orange like the tangerines.

23

After, I sat in coffee shop, ate tiny
bite of what is called here, in Japanese, of course, "Autumn ice cream
sundae."

Forest calls her "my emerald beauty" or "my
beautiful emerald."

His beautiful Emerald is not a cute and fragile
little kewpie doll. To set the woman down in a bou-
tique sale offering expensive fabrics or high-fashion
clothes or exotic kitchenware is to transmute her into
a howling samurai who can quite placidly skewer a
Bronx fishwife competitor. May twenty Shinto priests
have mercy on the fingers of any woman reaching for
that remnant of orange silk Emerald Hyashi Butler
intends to possess.

At times (until recently) their lovemaking has
benefited from the near-schizophrenia, the servant-
master drama, that prevails in their bedroom. Or
their living room. Or their kitchen or their garage or
their grape arbor. *Until recently* meaning these last few
months. Not so few, actually. Two? Three?

His own appetite having quite naturally declined
over the forty-two years since he was the word's
champion fifth-degree black belt adolescent mastur-
bator, Forest accepts without complaint Emerald's
less-frequent attentions these days (months) and, as
well, the diminution of her former on-call savagery.
Nature taking its course. Familiarity breeding its contempt. Passion that had been natural and familiar for
twenty years. *In relaxus*, as no one says in Latin.

Forest cannot recall when she last let him enter
her. Lately—the last three...four?—months, when he's
tried to insist, tried to force himself inside her, she
has been almost vicious in her resistance and her always—ultimately—successful denial. This last Thursday night, before his trip, in his most recent effort,
she'd even cursed him, after which she'd leaped out

of bed and rushed downstairs. He found her the next morning, wrapped in blankets, sleeping on the sofa.

But blessed be the god (goddess?) of fellatio. Emerald possesses a variety of exotic conceits that almost make Forest grateful for her current refusals. Her surprise gift these past nights: liberation from any need to dutifully reciprocate once he receives his pleasures. His routine half-hearted attempts are diverted or repelled with persuasive reassurance and loving kisses. *Relax, darling*. Nothing is expected of him. He has only to lie or sit or stand and be serviced. Who (what man?) would complain about that? You do not have to be Dr. Kinsey to know that, along the way, the very young Emerald Hayashi had to have been tutored well in the vocabulary of love, because her lean brown body speaks a variety of languages.

Since their marriage twenty years ago (thanks to the *New York Review of Books'* personal columns) Forest has rarely fantasized sex with other women, as he had when, as a lean and hungry and impoverished teaching assistant, one veal-faced coed replaced another in his night and day dreams. As a middle-aged tenured full-professor he has converted himself from an academic idealist into an academic realist. His attentions, especially during the current sabbatical, which just happened to coincide with the current sexual drought, have rooted themselves deeply in his Mark Twain research.

The anticipation of the explosion likely to occur when his article appears in the *Journal of American Literature* does, on occasion, excite him, even depositing an expanding family of tickles in his scrotum. Now and then, he finds his groin pulsating as it had on the best nights early in his marriage. As a member of a department famed for its lack of fame (until Farleigh O'Brien's victories in the Literary Sweepstakes) Forest, more than most of his colleagues, has gained a reputation, of sorts, that has led to local radio and

25

television commentators relying on him for occasional insights into contemporary American culture.

Maria Scarborough praises his ease before the cameras ("You ought to grow a beard and paste patches on the elbows of your jacket, Forest, and look like an academic. Maybe even take up a pipe."). Paul says Forest looks and sounds like a rustic Alistair Cook or, better, a suit-and-coated Falstaff. Emerald? Emerald only beams, and continues adding to her collection of videocassettes that already contain twelve of Forest's appearances on three different television stations.

Emerald Hayashi's offer of herself to the mail-order list of Asian Beauties has won her benefits most of the other Asian—and other "foreign" offerings—could only have dreamed of. One night, five years after her arrival at the San Francisco airport, following Forest's television commentary on the announcement that Wayne Newton was planning to direct a film of Mark Twain's *The Prince and the Pauper*, Emerald, who had taped her husband's display of bitter wit and fierce irony (the manager at the station had informed Forest that Newton had called and threatened to sue), had almost drawn and quartered him in bed. The sound that spilled from her throat spread across (he counted them) four octaves.

Forest was younger then, more amenable to idolatry. Older now, in his mid-fifties, he has begun to accept as inevitable the diminution of sexual gymnastics in both his wife and himself. He is beginning to adjust to his own secure tenure in the small-business portion of the education industry. After all, as in any job and with any couple, there are bound to be certain strains and stresses that convert former allure into acceptable boredom. Meetings. Libraries. Research. Teaching during the day, writing at night. Not, Forest has to concede, a dramatic life for a wife.

So, he is being as honest as he can be, not just charitable or generous, when—in his study, on a plane, in an inexpensive motel room in some dull town in Missouri—he admits to more than half of the responsibility for their current sexual armistice. He will do better, he promises himself (and Emerald, in absentia); he will give his beloved Emerald more attention, he will work to feed the almost insatiable hungers which, he is certain, still slumber in her loins.

Slumber in her loins. How biblical, Forest. Could you say Koranical? What is the Shinto text? Confuciunal?

He will make it up to Emerald. Should he consider a few of those sex aids so ostentatiously available these days? Perhaps a few XXX videos could add a pinch of spice into what must be, for Emerald, a bland and fading sex life. Now, look at that, would you? Just the thought of those videocassettes has deposited a surprising pool of heat in the somewhat jaded scrotum of Forest Butler.

Careful, Forest. Jaded scrotum is not a correct, let alone an appealing, image. The picture of his sac studded with sharp rhinestones sends chills between his buttocks, up along his spine.

And what if he were accosted by one of his students in one of those video shops?

"Hi, Professor Butler."

"Oh, hello, Marc. (Or John or Debby.) Sure, I come here regularly. I'm doing an article (a book, a lecture) on erotic literature. Oh, yes, I consider videocassettes to be literature. *Debbie Does Dallas?* Alliteration plays a major role in that cassette's success. *Behind the Green Door?* Interesting, Marc. Are you familiar with Lorca's line: 'Green, how I love you, green.'?"

This evening, he and Emerald will go out to dinner with Maria and Paul Scarborough. They will have a few drinks, they will probably hold hands. Tonight,

Emerald will slide into bed, will settle her head on his chest and, as accomplished as a geisha, will recite Li Po or Ji Li—haiku celebrating the wife's unwavering love for the husband, the master.

Hey! Tony Coniglio is calling at ten.

Emerald's association with Farleigh O'Brien consisted of a few department festivities, a few dinner exchanges in which Farleigh performed the role of a young angel come unto earth to dispense heavenly wisdom and spiritual enlightenment. She was impressed not just with his knowledge of Zen but his knowledge of the land of Japan in general, and the city of Kyoto in particular. How could an English professor/poet from Mill Valley, California, know so much? A man who has worn his Stetson and boots no more than a mile offshore in a commercial salmon trawler? How can Emerald Hyashi Butler be expected to appreciate the true O'Brien when she doesn't have to share a department and a career with the man?

"What is the word, Forest? For *angel?* That exhibit we see years ago. The painter. Long ago. Europe. Raphael." *Raphaerl.*

"The word? Let's see. In German or French or Hebrew?"

"You know. Naked. Round pink cheeks. Fat, cute. Little wings up here, on their shoulders. They fly."

"Ah. You mean the Dallas Cowboy Cheerleaders."

"Forest! It's...it's share...Share-ubs. He is like a share-ub. Farleigh O'Brien look like a shar-ub. Is it pronounced shar-ub? He look like a shar-ub."

"Looked. Past tense. He no longer looks like..."

"Stop it! Why you do this torture! That what you do to me. Torture."

As always, the more intense or incensed she is, the more she surrenders to the complexities of the

28

(to her) accursed language whose vowels and consonants assemble and split apart with the giddy aban-
don of sprouting weeds.

Emerald appears to have recovered when she
emerges from the bathroom. She has bathed and
changed into a robin's egg-blue silk blouse that deep-
ens the glow in her brown skin. A tight black skirt
displays the flat tummy and round, young-girl rump,
which has neither swollen nor dropped.

She has called Cafe Cerise, she informs Forest.
There are no tables available tonight, and the restaurant is accepting no reservations for at least two
months. Forest's groan is a wagging finger. Has she
forgotten that he had vowed, after their last meal
there, never to eat at Cafe Cerise again? The restaurant rests, he reminds her now as he had told her
then, on an initially well-earned but no longer deserved reputation.

"It's expensive, its servings are minute, its food is
over-rated by cowed critics, and its yuppy clientele
gives me constipation. Let's go Chinese."

They have almost unlimited choices in Berkeley's
gourmet ghetto, but Forest defers to Emerald, who
doesn't much care where they eat as long as, he suspects, the menu offers lamentation rare.

His diagnosis of his wife's current (meaning today's) mood: she's thinking of O'Brien's sudden de-
mise and her aged parents living alone in Kyoto.
She's frightened of death's reliance on surprise attacks. She wants to get out of the house, she wants to
be wined and dined, she wants to be pampered.

Well, why not? Why the hell not? Why should
Emerald be expected to savor the satisfaction he and
Paul Scarborough will earn by their volleying private
pleasures back and forth this evening like a shuttle-
cock in a badminton match sponsored by the
American Academic Asshole Association?

❧

The Scarboroughs, when they arrive, are delighted at Emerald's recommendation of Eve's Hunan on College Avenue. The prospect of ginger eggplant and mu shu pork, Maria purrs, makes her mouth water. Paul informs them all that the last time he was at Cafe Cerise he had almost punched out the waiter.

"I would have, too, if I'd been thirty years younger, forty pounds heavier, and black. No respectable hipyup waiter in Berserkeley would punch an angry black man."

"No drink," Emerald pleads. "We go right to restaurant."

The four of them, women in the rear, men in the front of Forest's red Toyota, ride down through the Berkeley hills and south along College Avenue to Eve's Hunan. Though the restaurant is always full, it offers a quick customer turnover and an almost homey atmosphere not available in too many Chinese restaurants. The hot onion cakes and spicy garlic eggplant appetizers will smooth the edges of Emerald's mood.

Once they order and Emerald pours tea, the Butlers and the Scarboroughs lean back in their chairs and then, as if at an agreed-upon silent signal, the two men bend closer. Paul Scarborough begins.

"Okay, we hated the bastard, but could you have predicted he'd kill himself?"

Emerald gasps. Forest reaches for her hand. Could she be sick? She appears more pale than usual, and the pain produced by Paul's remark does not seem feigned. Maria slaps her husband with an angry stare, caresses Emerald's face with an expression full of contrition or perhaps empathy.

Paul, before the two women, who have promptly joined emotional forces, can pounce upon him, adds, "Granted, granted. We didn't all hate him. In fact, everyone else, present company with two exceptions included, considers him a mix of Albert Schweitzer, Albert Einstein and Lassie. Hey! If he's an American Goethe, why don't I feel our culture, our college, and me, personally, all have suffered an enormous loss? Why do I feel relieved, almost pleased?"

"Because you're sick," his wife says. "And jealous."

Paul, the aggrieved innocent, arches his eyebrows and places the tip of an index finger against his chest. "Moi?"

Emerald plucks Forest's handkerchief out of the breast pocket of his Harris tweed jacket and presses it, without disturbing its folds, to her eyes. She uses the handkerchief with the skill of a marksman.

Maria Scarborough's eyes have already rolled toward the ceiling as her husband begins venting his now quite boring spleen; at least, Maria's groan and rolling blue eyes suggest boredom. Forest comes to the support of his friend and colleague. He would be saying relatively the same thing were he to have spoken out first, but now he can pose as a detached and honest observer reacting to a legitimate and perceptive judgment offered not just by a colleague but by one of the finest critical minds in the college. A mind, in certain important areas, equal and maybe even superior to his own.

"You didn't have to work with the man," Forest says. "You didn't have to watch them stand in line to lick his..."

"Forest!"

"Shoes. What's wrong with licking shoes, Em? The tradition goes back several hundred years at Eton."

The comment has been offered for the benefit of all, but only Paul seems grateful. In fact, Paul's grin almost bursts into a laugh. Trying to repair the domestic damage, Forest adds, "Please. I'm sorry to see any man die—okay, okay, any woman, too, I'm an equal opportunity sorrower—but, well, it's hard to generate pity or sympathy for..."

"An intellectual Ollie North."

Forest bursts out laughing. "Paul, where the hell did you get that? It's a perfect metaphor."

Emerald shakes her head. "I not sit here and ret you...Forest, I said I did not want you and Paul to crucify Farreigh O'Brien. Not tonight. You do it in office, on campus. Okay? Not home. Not dinner. Not tonight."

"My dear, you said you hoped we'd not be bitchy. There's a big difference."

"I won't stay if both you be..."

"Honest?"

"Forest, you trying to make me reave? I will. I warn you."

"Dishonest?"

Maria reaches over to cup Emerald's hand in her own. "Emerald, forgive them. They know not what they do. They're insanely jealous of Farleigh's talents and successes. For years, they've shared secret plans to kill him, but neither of them has the guts. Heaped together, they don't have enough courage to throw a spitball. Farleigh's death has denied them their adolescent pleasure."

Forest waits for Paul to rescue him, but Paul seems almost happy to indulge his wife her nasty little female digs. Forest shakes his head. Though neither of the women nor anyone else—well, very damn few—could ever appreciate his or Paul's sentiments, Maria's barb has struck home.

He has to admit that, secretly but frequently, he has, indeed, wondered about both the intensity and the duration of his own anger. Not only has his anger never gone away, it has never thinned. It has, if anything, bloomed into obsession. Is he jealous? Are his and Paul Scarborough's perceptions of the man-professor-poet-critic born not of legitimate critical assessment but of cheap garden-grade jealousy?

A gulp of hot coffee agitates an idea that could be considered explosive. A scholar explores his perceptions by writing about them, by publishing them, by rousing support for them. Will Forest Butler be the first of Farleigh O'Brien's colleagues to write about Farleigh O'Brien?

Both hands press his forehead, as if the idea adds so much weight the vertebrae in his neck require extra support. Whoever had conceived the term *atlas* for that first cervical vertebrae had to have been a poet. A male poet.

Back to the book. The book!

A book! There has to be a book. Not just a book, but a novel. It has to be a novel. It has to be a novel about college, about students and professors, about the tyranny of poetry, about contemporary poets riding the lecture circuits, sharing first-class flights with CEOs and news commentators and athletes and momentary right- and left-wing political heroes.

Has there ever been a rollicking good academic novel? No. A novel, by definition, must not be academic. Academic writing guarantees specialized, self-serving, dead-eyed readers, and no more of those than can be counted on one finger. Fiction writers who cannot drop their academic persona? Booooooring! Samples: Bellow. Roth. See the professors lecturing, see the professors parading their intelligence, see the professors converting textbook-called-fiction into true-life dollars. See the dollars flowing like a green flood into checking and savings accounts and stocks and bonds.

A novel *about* academics? Better, that's better. But even a novel about academics will have a potential publisher's cold commercial eye cast upon it. Readers? Profits? How many readers out there among what Menken called the booboisee? How many readers out there will shell out twenty-five dollars for a novel about a professor-poet? To care about a professor, you have to care about teaching. And no more than one resident in twenty-four households in every state in the union respects teaching or teachers. If you can't be a plumber or an electrician or a clerk or a salesman, okay, you can always be a teacher.

A good academic novel. An oxymoron for morons. A novel *about* academia?

Let's see. There is *Groves of Academe*. Mary McCarthy. Old. The book, not Mary. Mary's dead now, but the book's death had preceded her bodily surrender. A prissy Ivy League kitchen cynic. A lowrider in the high lecture circuit. "A brilliant but snotty elitist," the director of Berkeley's art-and-lecture series had informed Forest. McCarthy had apparently demanded enormous fees and then deigned to speak for twenty-four minutes, after which, and refusing to accept questions, she'd left the stage and entered a cab for the airport, fare paid by the university.

How about *Lucky Jim*? Better, much better. As current now as when it was written—what? forty years ago? Kingsley Amis. Yes, *Lucky Jim* might be a model. He will have to take a look at *Jim* again.

Trading Places. David Lodge. Contemporary. Original. A perfect portrait. A bit flip, a bit slick but funnier than hell. Also British. Pages of truth truth truth but, again, more British than American.

Farleigh O'Brien, despite the Irish name, is pure contemporary...was purely American. The purest of contemporary me-first-I-want-it-all-and-I-want-it-now New Age Californians. This novel about such a hero will have to smell of comic Twain with a twist-of-a-rind-scent of morbid-moody Faulkner. And who better to write such a novel than the college's resident Twain scholar and Faulkner devotee, Forest—

Paul Scarborough, studying Forest's face, is grinning like the Cheshire cat practicing before Tenniel's arrival.

"You're the one to do it," Paul murmurs.

"To do what?" Maria asks. She looks to Forest for help and then to Paul and then she looks wearily at Emerald, shaking her head as if to deny the insight she has happened upon. "Sweet Jesus," she says. "They're going to write a book about Farleigh's death."

"Suicide," Paul says.

"Maybe," Forest says.

Maria, were a flame-thrower available, would inflame her husband's thinning hair.

Emerald considers Maria's statement as if the words have no meaning, as if she is in the throes of a translation conflict.

"A book?"

"A book," Maria repeats, "full of fury, signifying nothing."

"Not a book," Paul Scarborough says. "You can't write a book about Farleigh O'Brien. You have to write a novel. Only professors will read a book. And Farleigh O'Brien belongs to..."

"...the people," Forest says. His turn not to grin but to laugh. "And to posteriority."

Paul, with a wink of approbation, cocks thumb and forefinger and aims his mock gun at Forest.

"That goes into your novel."

Maria Scarborough and Emerald Hayashi Butler sigh in chorus and, as if reacting to a too-often-rehearsed joke, close their eyes. To open them when the first round of dishes arrives.

Why, at this moment, does Forest think of Bonnie O'Brien? One single victim out of the universe's rapidly filling reservoir of long-suffering wives. Why Bonnie now?

If he eventually writes the novel—not if but when (when meaning soon, meaning now, meaning tonight)—when he starts writing the novel, he will have to talk to Bonnie. Not an unattractive assignment. Beautiful, long-legged, always-tanned, full-mouthed, Balinese-dancer-titted, cynical Bonnie. Is that why she comes to mind now? Here at Eve's Hunan? Now, with the delivery of the spicy carp, the memory of that night they—the O'Briens and the Butlers—had come here to...

⮑

Forest and Emmy had invited the O'Briens to this restaurant to celebrate O'Brien's appointment to the faculty of Saint Catherine's. They had shared the baked and crisp and spicy whole carp. Farleigh had received compliments from the waiter for his facility with the chopsticks, and ever the adept enchanter, Farleigh had responded with a few phrases of gratitude in Mandarin. When the waiter praised his accent, Bonnie had volunteered to Emerald and Forest the information that Farleigh had approximately twenty such phrases available in ten languages, should he have occasion to impress editors or interviewers—or college hiring committees.

"Or," she added, as postscript, "graduate students."

Though her voice contained a suggestion of coolth, Farleigh had not demonstrated discomfort. In fact, Farleigh had smiled serenely, as if his learning and versatility included graduate degrees in the practice of Christian indulgence.

⮑

Forest fumbles for Emerald's hand to demonstrate the effectiveness of the waitress's perfume, but Emerald pulls her hand free before he can take her fingers and (an always titillating ploy at restaurants or dinner parties) cup them over the bulge in his trousers.

No matter. This is like that one and only night he smoked marijuana with a student. His senses are honed to their finest fiber. He can separate and appreciate each herb and condiment applied to the sizzling-rice soup, the oyster-asparagus, the carp.

Paul wants to linger after dinner, but Forest says he is expecting an important phone call from one of his contacts in Missouri and must be home before nine o'clock.

"Champing at the bit, Forest? Good luck, friend."

Paul Scarborough raises both hands, two fingers on each of them crossed.

⁓

The phone is ringing when Forest enters the kitchen from the basement stairs. He rushes into his study while Emerald, having preceded him, continues down the hall to the bathroom.

"Yo, Forest. Tony here."

"Thanks for calling back, Tony. Can you tell me..."

"The Farleigh O'Brien suicide. What I know about it. Right?"

"That's it. So, it was suicide."

"We can't say for sure. Look, I can't, you know, talk about the case. The investigation's ongoing."

"What would you guess—if you were a gambling man, of course—what would you say the odds are against his having killed himself?"

"Look, man, you know, this is day one. Two of my guys are new, right out of the academy. Give us a break. Okay? I'll call you tomorrow night or the next night. A suggestion: don't go betting big money he shot himself. You know? Okay? Give my love to Emerald, man."

37

The implications make Forest woozy. What is Tony implying? What does he know? How much of what he knows will—can—he confide to his old professor, current friend?

Patience, Forest.

To woo back Emerald's sympathies, Forest does not refer again that evening, or afterwards, in bed, to Farleigh O'Brien's suicide. Nor does he try to make love to her. He knows her too well. When, with a gentle hand, he rubs the lovely and so aptly named Venus mound, and the crisp, curly pubic hair crinkles inside her silk nightgown, and he says, "I love you," her body shifts away. He adds, "I'm sorry, daring. I just never realized Farleigh O'Brien meant so much to you."

Only then does her hand drop onto his erection and hold it, not with desire or affection, but with resignation. As if, by shifting it right and left, back and forward, she, the conscientious pilot merely doing her job, can control his slow descent into sleep. Why the erection? Her scent? That blue silk blouse? The apricot nightgown? That fine young-girl rump? The first erotic teasings of the now inescapable determination to get to work on a novel?

That! That's it !

Not reading or teaching fiction but writing fiction is, for Forest Butler, the great aphrodisiac. What had La Coste said about Cervantes? When satisfied with his day's work at the desk he was capable at night of bedding a woman for an hour; when extremely satisfied it was two or three women, for several hours. When exultant: multitudes of women day after day.

≈

Forest sets the alarm not for the usual seven o'clock but for six. The extra hour will be devoted to his beginnings. First chapter, first paragraph, first sentence six o'clock tomorrow morning.

As he closes his eyes and stretches out in the bed, ideas gallop through his mind like a flock of unruly sheep. He resists the urge to count them.

Though always a light sleeper, he does not wake up when Emerald slips out of bed at three a.m., and again at five, first to swallow two aspirins and, later, a Valium. Forest is so deeply asleep he is not at all aware of his wife lying on her side, resting her head on her hand, observing him. And weeping.

CHAPTER 3

When the alarm buzzes, Forest keeps his eyes closed, fumbles for the switch, turns it off. Emerald does not stir. Legs straight out, arms at his side, Forest remains in bed, savoring that tingle of excitement he has known only twice before in his life, those two brief detours around his daily, hourly regimen of academic polemic.

This morning, tonight, next week, in his redwood-paneled study, he will be relying on his imagination, on his unpredictable and almost unlimited imagination. He will not be studying brittle newspapers, stained magazines, blurred microfilm cached in libraries and museums and warehouses designed by the Department of Prisons.

The challenge of confronting his creative instead of his scholarly instincts sustains a rapture never available in the production of banal articles destined to be read by the editor of the appointed journal and three or four other professors searching for justification for their own articles (on the same topic) in their own appointed journals to be read by the editor of their own...One sharp exchange of credible dialogue proves more gratifying than a dozen footnoted references to arcane texts composed by mildewed fellow-pedants. Perhaps two or three of the rest of America's two hundred thousand scholars possess such quality—high quality—creative instincts (what Joshua Lowenfels calls "not just the will to be God but the skill.").

God. My creation.

First the heavens created He...

For both of his earlier novels Forest had used the pseudonym Frank Ryder, the name of the uncle who had held him hostage to fireside stories. As a child at his Uncle Fred's feet, Forest Butler had learned to gallop with leathery, mustachioed cowboys and Pony Express riders up and down mountain trails and across prairies filled with herds of buffalo and howling Apaches and cut-throat rustlers. Without ever leaving the house.

After his first and then his second novel had been rejected by numerous publishers, Forest, in secret and in silence, accepted his punishment for straying. He'd never been tempted to stray a third time.

Until today. Until this morning. Until six hours ago. Until now.

But even now, in bed, he recognizes the faintest... faintest what? Guilt? Anxiety? Desperation?

He has to admit he owes those scorned libraries and lecture halls a fair share of gratitude for a comfortable life these last thirty years. The night the final remaining copy of the second novel joined the final remaining copy of the first novel in the flames—ten? eleven? twelve years ago?—Forest had vowed he would remain satisfied (if not satisfied, at least at peace) with his small wedge of territory located in the subcontinent of American Letters: the Life and Times of Mark Twain, with an occasional two-lane road leading south and east to Yoknapotapha County, Mississippi, and wily Willy Faulkner.

But oh! those heady surges of almost sexual excitement not just as he had written those two failed novels but, and especially, as he had thought and dreamed about them before one word was placed on paper and then as words followed other words. Not a hint of such exhilaration had ever accompanied the routine tours through dozens of libraries and hundreds of bibliographies and thousands of footnotes for—as he'd described them to the sympathetic Paul Scarborough—his academia nuts.

Thanks to the humbling consequences of the intellectual jogging—the library research, the dreary seminars, the paying or pretending to pay obeisance to the latest critical fads and fashions, the dissertations, the orals, the grudging respect for the publish-or-perish laws that govern even Saint Catherine's—thanks to all of that, Forest Butler, ten (or eleven or twelve) years ago, at the approximate age of forty five, had resigned himself to his fate. He would remain a critic of American literature instead of a writer of it, a citizen on the curb, admiring and reporting on the passing parade of American culture.

Now, in bed, for a brief moment, Forest's creative urges...

Wait a moment, wait a moment! What is this?

Sometime during the night, Emerald had thrown her left arm about Forest's abdomen and had settled her cheek on his chest. She is especially appealing now, her small, smooth yellow-brown body lying atop his white hairy body like an oriental undine just washed up by the tide, face still marked with clots of black seaweed, a partial web of the glossy stuff stretched across her cheek. Long black eyelashes quiver as she struggles to remain asleep. Her delicate bird-boned body is so nearly weightless that her right leg shifting slightly is a feather brushing his thigh. Faint sucking sounds escape Emerald's pink mouth as she tries in her sleep to clear her throat.

How innocent, how vulnerable. He will take her now, quickly, fiercely, and later she will confess her pretense—she'd been awake, waiting, hoping for just such an assault, feigning innocence while possessed by desire.

But what if she is not pretending? What if she awakens as he mounts her? Or what if, defying his desire, she rolls over, giving him her discretely muscled back, and remains asleep?

Back or backside. Rear entry is never easy for Emerald. Small and tight, she requires gentle and patient persuasion and creamed preparation. But Forest does not, must not, feel gentle this morning. His conquest must be intense, explosive. He doesn't give a damn at this moment about her pleasure, he wants only his own and he wants it to be thunderous.

Paul's voice booms from the shadows of memory: "Fiction, Forest, is risk."

To hell with you, Paul. This is Emerald, this is my beloved wife. No risk here. Emerald loves me, I love Emerald. Emerald is my savior. Save me, Emerald.

His hand floats above the barely available left nipple. As if in deceitful collusion, Emerald shivers slightly, her buttocks tightening and quivering. When she rolls about, to nuzzle his chest, her hair gives off the faint scent of lilac, her breath warms the skin of his throat. With the gentlest of pressure he pulls her cheek into the hair on his chest. He can easily convince both her and himself, should the gambit fail, that he has assumed, attempted, nothing.

❦

The early Emerald had learned to accept and then appreciate and finally gorge herself on the presence of Forest's body hair. Only after two years of marriage had she confided to him that among her Kyoto friends and relatives a man with such a deposit of hair on torso or face would be considered crude, the lowest of the low, undesirable, uncultured.

She has told him several times since then that, acclimated finally to this contrasting culture—yang embracing yin, negative-positive poles merging—the presence of hair, especially on his chest and back, can send her to heights never experienced even in her dreams. At the peak of arousal she frequently chews on his nipples, sounding like a starved and possibly rabid mink. Her teeth have torn out clumps of his hair and, more than once, flesh.

Not for weeks. Months?

Not this morning. Emerald is not pretending, she is not being coy, she is asleep.

A little twitch, like a warning bell, strikes somewhere inside Forest's mind. To pursue, to advance, to attempt penetration would be a gamble with demeaning side effects if he's rebuffed. But remember, Forest, risk is part of this new adventure. How better to start this first morning than with defiance of risk? He recalls that silly hippy motto of the now-contemptible sixties: Today is the first day of the rest of your life.

Goddamn it, Forest, do it!

No. First things first. He will not gamble. Not this morning. There will be other mornings.

And so, at four minutes past six, Forest frees his thighs of Emerald's legs, slides his chest from under her cheek, carefully eases his limbs out of bed. He permits himself one moment to regret that there is not a sign or sound of protest from his oriental sea-nymph.

He pulls on his new pure-white terrycloth robe. He goes into his study, sits at his computer. He contemplates the blank screen for a moment and then his fingers, moved by a spirit he will only later call instinct, taps out the word *murder* and the word *metaphor*. On impulse he capitalizes both and inserts *or* between them.

Murder or Metaphor. Impression? Doctrinaire, pedantic. *Murder or Metaphor.* Life or death. It could be shouted by Patrick Henry. "Give me murder or give me metaphor." He deletes the *or* and replaces it with *by* so that now it reads *Murder by Metaphor.*

"The ripe fruit," he will inform Paul Scarborough that afternoon, only partly in jest, "of the cultivated, fertilized, harvested creative instinct of Forest Butler."

Forest, Paul will advise, sounds like a sophomore student in a creative writing workshop.

"Lord God, if you call it *ripe fruit* before you've finished the first chapter what will it be when the last chapter comes round? Rotten kiwi?"

But Paul will admit that—ripe fruit or rotten kiwi—he will forever envy Forest.

"You have more guts than I do, old friend. We who are about to die salute you who are about to live. You crazy bastard, I wish I could brag about some of that so-called creative instinct. Tell you a secret—sometimes I even envy Danielle Steele."

Instinct has never played a role in Forest's academic writings (*Twain's Bitter Vision; American Wars and Their Fiction; The Dark Sides of Faulkner's Moons; Race and Reality in American Fiction*), but now instinct brazenly takes over, a provocative guest moving in to stay forever in the most attractive and most comfortable bedroom in the house.

Forest centers the three words, alters the type to Courier, font to 12, italic to straight. And without plan he makes it bold. **Murder by Metaphor.**

A title!

The title! The whole thing, the entire novel, the life and death of Farleigh O'Brien—poet, professor, culture-god, evil incarnate (a phrase that has traveled with

Forest from his eighth-grade readings about Hitler)—the whole novel lives in the horizontal collection of these sixteen letters.

Forest types without pausing to think or even stretch for the next fifty-five minutes. Lines, fragments, phrases, sentences, images, ideas, paragraphs, unbound packages of words. When he hears the alarm buzz in the bedroom and hears Emerald clear her throat, he takes a deep breath, saves everything and shoves back his chair. He almost shouts at the burst of pride inside his chest and the after-slide of that pride into relief as satisfying as any orgasm he has ever experienced.

He pauses, thinking, Men (women?) don't remember orgasms. They remember the details that led up to and away from those orgasms—the walk in the moonlight, the canoe ride across the lake, the rain beating the window, the cold floor, the flames in the fireplace. Example (he thinks): that most recent orgasm with Emerald that followed the appearance of the nightgown she was wearing, that followed the summer-meadow scent of her body, that followed the tenderness of the palm of her hand at his sac, that followed the sounds of her lips and tongue favoring the lathered head.

Now, from the bedroom, comes Emerald's yawn. He moves to interrupt her passage from bed to bathroom, but she moves too fast. He hears the bathroom door close, the toilet flush, the shower strike the tiled walls.

He glides downstairs on a rail of self-worship.

Forest makes breakfast while Emerald bathes and dresses. Before he sets the table and drops the bread into the toaster, he goes to the front door. A heavy mist that had reluctantly decided not to be rain pushes against his face. He picks up the cellophane-wrapped *San Francisco Chronicle*. Farleigh O'Brien is not headline material this morning, but he is still front page—two columns, left side ("continued on back page, see Poet suicide.")

Forest resists the temptation to torment himself or to tease or confuse the still-hovering muses by trying to read the news before or while preparing breakfast. He will wait until Emerald leaves for work, then read at his leisure. Breakfast now. Emerald now. Then, after Emerald leaves for San Francisco and he reads the latest details, he will return to *Murder by Metaphor*, and he will resist the temptation to inform Paul of the details.

When he is well into the pages—say, let's see, at page 200...yes, at page 200—he will show the manuscript to Paul then, before Paul's critical comments can compel him to change so much as a single punctuation mark.

The Irish steel-cut oatmeal has been cooking in nonfat milk instead of water. He adds a tablespoon of molasses, a tablespoon of honey, a handful of black raisins, a pat of butter, some chopped walnuts.

He fills Emerald's bowl.

The *Chronicle* is lying on the breakfast table folded, the O'Brien story on the underside, when Emerald kisses his cheek and sits in her chair, facing the west so she might have her early-morning view of the bay and the fog-shrouded city of San Francisco. She avoids the newspaper, giving her attention instead to her bowl of cereal. She smiles as she chews, nodding her beautiful black-haired head.

"Forest, this best you ever make."

"Thank you, me proud beauty."

Instead of the usual single piece of toast with her tea, she has two. And then a third. She is either ignoring or has forgotten her sworn commitment to reduced calorie consumption.

"I'll be home a bit late tonight, Forest. You make supper, please? Something light. Maybe just a salad?"

"I'll manage. Trust me. A meeting at the office?"

"Yes. Bigelow is afraid the Feds will find something bad. So we double check every document, every ledger, every penny."

"Let's see. Two million dollars amounts to— what?— two billion pennies?"

"He is worried. He does not have to worry. Everything is correct."

Forest, after Emerald descends the interior stairs, opens the basement-garage doors and drives off in her blue coupe, returns to the kitchen. Then, to the sofa with, under his arm, the *Chronicle*, and in his hands a tray containing buttered toast, a jar of orange marmalade, a small bowl of oatmeal, a small carafe of hot coffee.

The *Chronicle*, page two—a smaller version of yesterday's photograph. Foul play has been ruled out in the death of Farleigh O'Brien...

Foul play has been ruled out...

Foul play has been...

The newspaper drops to the floor. No! Foul play has decidedly *not* been ruled out in the death of Farleigh O'Brien. Foul play has just been ruled *in*. Lord Forest Butler, having created sin, now has to create a sinner. Or sinners, plural.

He almost runs to the computer, the hands of his memory holding a shadow-wrapped memory of a young undergraduate student reading aloud—"Ash Wednesday," "Four Quartets," "Pisan Cantos"—and a supportive memory of himself, after hours of listening, mimicking the voices of poets reading their own works on those Caedmon classics.

In his mind's ear now, the dreary sepulchral cadences of Eliot, the slippery arrogant whine of Pound. Had either Eliot or Pound remained awake until early morning at their desks, composing their examinations of sorrow? Had either Eliot or Pound wept at their lost ideals, their tarnished loves? Had

Eliot or Pound ever even *had* ideals? Had Eliot, Pound ever loved anyone but themselves? Will there be—five years from now, this novel published and praised and paying for an early retirement—as there had been for Eliot and Pound, a cult that follows every word of Forest Butler, that sage of Berkeley, California?

Not likely. Will Forest Butler find admirers bowing, doffing their poetic caps, tugging their metaphorical forelocks, surrounding him with praise? Should Forest grow a beard, wear a beret, take up the pipe? Cultivate a British accent. He pounds away at key after key after key on the magnificent compu—the telephone!

Two rings. Three rings. Damn it, he'd forgotten to turn off the ringer. Then, thinking it might be important news from Paul, he rushes to the desk.

"Yo, Forest."

"Yes, this is For...hey, Tony!"

"Forest, do you know if O'Brien was right-handed or left-handed? Or was he, what do you call it? Either one."

"Ambidextrous."

"I never remember the word. It sounds dirty."

"Let me think. He was...wait a minute...he was right-handed. Yeah, I'm sure of it. Right-handed."

"Do me a favor, will you, man?"

"Sure."

"Pretend you have a pistol—a thirty-eight special—in your right hand. Just pretend."

"Okay, though I haven't the slightest idea what a thirty-eight special looks like."

"No sweat. Just pretend it's a capgun. You holding it? In your right hand?"

"Yeah."

"Bring the weapon up to shoot yourself in your temple."

50

Forest does as directed.

"Now which temple—left or right—is your weapon aimed at?"

"My right temple."

"Now, keeping the weapon in your right hand try to shoot yourself in your left temple."

Impossible. If you were right-handed and wanted to shoot yourself you'd put the gun to your right temple.

"Did the papers say where he shot himself, Forest?"

"Yes. In the left temple. Tony?"

"Yeah?"

"Why'd you call me?"

"Well, I don't know, man. Poets are strange, you know. The city of San Francisco's full of them, and they're all wackos. You're a professor, you knew O'Brien. Maybe you can give me some information."

"Do you have a suspect, Tony?"

"Nothing yet. We're operating on what's called speculation. But I want to ask you something. We've been doing, you know, some preliminary stuff. Turns out that on the morning of O'Brien's death Professor Scarborough, Professor Lederberg, Professor Goldstein were all in San Francisco.

"Professor Lederberg had an appointment at UC Hospital. A friend drove her over here to the city. Too sick to drive herself. Professor Scarborough told me to go to hell when I asked him why he was in San Francisco, but I know he was picking up a daughter named...let's see...named Nina, home for holiday from college.

"Professor Goldstein and Brother Charles were meeting with the Provincial about college issues. Goldstein. Never had Professor Goldstein at Saint Cate's. He's retiring next year. He's sixty-eight. No, he's sixty-nine. Hey, you weren't in San Francisco, too, were you? Who the hell was watching the store at Saint Cate's?"

51

"Tony, you bastard, I was in Missouri. I caught a three o'clock flight out of San Francisco. Want to see my ticket stub? You don't suspect one of those three—Lederberg, Scarborough, Goldstein—do you? Or me."

"I don't have any suspects, Forest. Honest to God. In fact, we can't say for the record yet that it's even homicide. I just start at the beginning and work my way toward the end."

"Right."

"As soon as I know anything I'll call you, okay?"

"Tony, I appreciate it."

"Hey, you gave Tony Coniglio the only A he ever got in college. I owe you at least two more favors. Remember. I'm waiting for an invite to dinner. Emerald still makes the best sushi and tempura in the country?"

"She does, indeed. I'll talk to her. We'll set a date."

"Later, man."

"Later," Forest says. He sets the phone in place and returns to his tray and the *Chronicle*, but he remains distracted by a concern, almost a suspicion, about Tony's call. What does Tony have to gain from letting Forest know he has three names he is checking out? There is no official decision yet about whether Farleigh is a victim of suicide or homicide. Did he call just to keep Forest, his professor, his friend, updated?

It doesn't matter. Here, just now, served on a telephonic platter, gratis, is the basic plot for *Murder by Metaphor*.

In bold: **Murder by Metaphor**. And—get this, Paul—also served on that telephonic platter: a theme.

Theme? The theme of *Murder by Metaphor*? Poetry kills. *Kills*. The word itself takes him on as an ally in its vulgar menace. Is he, Forest Butler, a killer? Could he, Forest Butler, kill? Does he, Forest Butler, *want* to kill? Even in a made-up, imaginary, pretend collection of words that form what is called a novel?

For a moment—Forest is unprepared for this shocking wave of regret that comes washing over him so suddenly. For just a moment, Forest considers giving it up, deserting this new ship. Regret washes in and through and over him.

Farleigh O'Brien does not deserve the scorn his death will be receiving in this novel.

Farleigh succumbed to temptations that destroyed him. A man ten—twelve? fifteen?—years younger than Forest, a human being Forest had once respected if not admired, is dead. A meaningful piece of his own life has ended, will soon be—is already—only memory. If there is one lesson learned in thirty years of research into the lives of Twain and Faulkner that lesson is that memory can never be trusted. No one's memory. Not even his own.

The *Chronicle* photograph catches Forest's eye again, and the regret he feels for the loss of a colleague, a friend, an artist, gives way to an anger that morphs into, of all things, a sense of victory. Think of the words: *the heart surges.*

It happens.

Forest's heart surges.

Forest Butler's heart surges. An arm seems to reach out from the sky, its hand cups his ass and tosses him aloft. He has the sensation a gull or hawk must experience when riding a spring thermal. He is alive.

Forest Butler is alive. Forest Butler is sitting here at his computer writing a novel. Lord God, feel that surge that is greater, more exhilarating, than any remembered surge of any episode that might be called lust.

Lust!

Just you wait, Emerald Hyashi Butler, just you wait. When you get home tonight you are going to get it.

I am writing again. I am writing a novel again. A Murder Mystery that will not be a mystery!

Exactly what every New York publisher demands these days. How can this novel be anything but a scream of success!

Forest Butler. Professor Forest Butler. No, no. Forget the Professor. Forest Butler, the author.

Forest Butler, the author of that international best-seller *Murder by Metaphor*. *Murder by Metaphor*. The novel soon to be a movie. Hollywood. Cannes.

Hurry home, Emerald!

CHAPTER 4

Forest spends the afternoon in his study, trying to concentrate on the Twain material he brought from Missouri, but he is distracted by that gray-boxed extraterrestrial called the computer.

"Wait," said Paul Scarborough, the techy-god. "In the next year or two your computer will be able to create a poem Byron or Keats would envy or a novel Stendahl would have offered if he'd lived till today. Just press the Create Novel key and sit back."

Forest waved him away. "You've had too many martinis, Paul. Fiction comes from blood and guts, not from wires and keys and plastic. You have to live life to create life. That's why scholars never make credible novelists."

"Sorry to offend," Paul said. "Mea mya culpa. You're the novelist. I defer, *mein Fuhrer. Ich bin* mighty stupido."

Forest, tippy-tapping words onto the screen, cannot help, every now and then now, pausing to imagine the completed manuscript in his hands. He slows, pauses, crosses his arms on his chest.

Take your time, Forest. Trust your creative impulses. Creative impulses. Sounds like that wacko psych instructor who lectured the faculty last year on Psyche is Soul.

Take your time, Forest. Be patient, Forest. This novel can be important, can bring you the fame every scholar will envy, Forest. And attack.

Look at this vision just arrived—such a vision would never have appeared were he at work on his Twain material. See these gnarled old professors emeriti, crossing the hundreds of American campuses on their way to their offices in the libraries, limping their way along the memorized routes like slat-ribbed old mine ponies continuing to plod in circles through the green fields of their retirement, their milky eyes seeing neither green grass nor bright sunlight nor black cave walls.

Forest sits back, arms crossed over his chest. Not bad, Forest, not bad, considering the fact you've never seen a mine-pony or lived within a thousand miles of a coal mine.

But you have never sailed a steamboat or floated on a barge or navigated the Mississippi River, either, and look at you. You are the American Twain-expert. You never met a Southerner, man or woman, until you were fifty years old, but even Paul considers you a Faulkner Scholar.

When this novel is published, Forest Butler will wash out his mouth every time he uses the word *scholar*.

Give it up, Forest. Permit this creative spirit a moment's rest.

He makes himself a cup of coffee, carries cup-on-saucer into the living room. His favorite room. For Emerald, each of the seven rooms is "...my favorite room." Oh, my beloved Emerald!

He remembers Emerald dancing into the bathroom her first day, her first ten minutes, in this house:

"White tub rlarge as poorl for swim...swing...swim...lie in, move rleft foot, right foot up, down."

Now, this evening, the house is bright with light from the sun pausing a moment in its descent onto San Francisco Bay and the Golden Gate Bridge and the green hills of Marin County. Like the rest of the house, the walls and ceilings are slabs of redwood. Fumes expelled by four generations of residents have darkened the original deep-red tones to an almost glossy mahogany. An old house but not as old as the Scarboroughs'. The Scarborough house is a large, almost grotesquely baroque Victorian moved in the early twenties on joined barges across the Bay from San Francisco, then roped and chained and winched up across the Berkeley hills into a protective grove of eucalyptus trees.

"More early-American sculpture than house," Paul claims.

Emerald will turn this house five months after Forest dies (he will be eighty, she will be sixty), into a West Coast Shinto temple, with burning incense adding scented gloss to the redwood.

This house, the purchase of it, was the riskiest decision Forest ever made. His wisest decision ever?

No. His wisest decision ever: the mailing of that fifty-dollar check to *The New York Review of Books* for the list—(in the three pages of Personals Ads of Men Seeking Women, Women Seeking Men, Great Danes Seeking Cocker Spaniels, Fallen Arches Seeking Podiatrists)—of Asian-Women-Seeking-American-Men. The arrival of Emerald Hyashi has brought comfort and joy to this house which, without Emerald Hyashi, would now be nothing more than a repository for Forest Butler's aging bones and clogging arteries.

Stop it, Forest.

57

Don't go there. Don't even wonder where *where* is or what's there. Fight off this goddamn self-pity, Forest, or write poetry about it and be appointed poet-laureate and earn a Nobel Prize and...

The gospel according to Saint Paul the Scar: in the last ten years, the practitioners of contemporary American poetry, with a crude, shrewd obsession reminiscent of Byzantine church politicians, have been engaged in machinations that have altered laws, manipulated political grants, foundations, magazines and readings; have rifled the souls and wallets of millions of lost and gullible throb-seekers out there in wooze-soaked America. The rewards to the reigning kings and queens and princes (and, now, in 1993, its princesses) have, voila! created a cottage industry. *Murder by Metaphor* will offer Forest Butler a chance to vent his own spleen on scholars and poets, all those politicians from Eros, all those (to use Paul Scarborough's venom) intellectual Ollie Norths.

Six o'clock. Dinnertime. Forest lets the phone ring five times before answering.

"Forest," Emerald says, "the funerarl. Farreigh O'Brien. It tomorrow." No space or time for the verb?

"On a Saturday? There's supposed to be a storm on Saturday. Anyway, that's fast, isn't it? Forty-eight hours?"

"I call Bonnie. She say...she says Farreigh brother making arrangements." A deep breath to gather energy and verbal-control. "Bonnie and Dyranna wir be there."

"Dylanna's a woman by now. I haven't seen her for..."

"Dyranna seventeen. Bonnie say she suffer much."

"Why should she suffer? She didn't especially like her father."

"Forest, that rong ago. Dyranna a responsibere young woman now."

"Like all the seventeen-year-olds we know. Right? Right. Anyway, I presume we'll be there."

Another deep breath, control secure now.

"Of course, we will be there. It is Saint Catherine chapel. You call Scarboroughs? We should probably go in one car. The traffic and parking will be heavy."

"Highway Thirty-six? On a Saturday? For Farleigh O'Brien's funeral? Come on, love, he's not Willie Nelson, you know, or Nelson Mandela. What time?"

"Three. Afternoon."

"I'll call Paul and Maria. I suspect I'm not to wear jeans."

In the long silence, he can hear the sounds of her deliberations, like belts creaking. He waits. Should I ignore him, she is asking herself, or should I serve up a special condemnation in Japanese?

"I'll wear my go-to-burial suit and I'll polish my shoes. What time will you be home this evening, my lovely? I'll go to Pacific Sea Food for fresh salmon. How's the audit going?"

"Fine. I be home seven." Click.

Pissed. Royally, righteously pissed, as only Emerald of the royal house of Hyashi can be pissed.

Two minutes later, settled again before the computer, Forest has forgotten the call. *Murder by Metaphor* rises up like an ancient warrior intent on defeating clock and calendar. When the alarm he'd set after Emerald's call goes off at six-forty-five he phones Paul Scarborough at home.

"Paul?"

"Forest, you should have been at the college today. The campus is in turmoil."

"You know the funeral's tomorrow?"

"Right. I was about to call and suggest we go in one car. There will be a bigger cavalcade coming over the bridge from Berkeley and the city than hit us when the pope visited Saint Catherine's. All of our colleagues here are in tears. Achilles has been slain by Hector. The finest mind, the most golden of tongues, has been silenced. The greatest American poet since Eliot...etcetera etcetera etfuckingcetera."

"I think you and I are the only ones who consider Eliot neither British nor American. *Neutral* was your word."

"Wrong, friend. My word was *neutered*. He—Eliot, that is is—was, will be—not much more than a dapper old queen who could would never fart. Read Cynthia Ozick's essay on the pompous little bastard. I wonder if ol' Tom El-liot..." Paul refuses to use the single l, calling it a fashionable tic, like cummings' lower case. "...will welcome Farleigh up there to that great poetry reading in the sky. Can't you hear him? 'You were foolish to do away with yourself, dear boy. In another ten or fifteen years you would surely have won the Nobel Prize in Puttery. I know the authorities up here. Could have pulled some strings for you. Concocted a minor miracle, I could have.'"

"Tell me, Paul. Who would kill Farleigh O'Brien? Pick a character and a motive."

"Kill? You're having him killed? You're writing a thriller? A mystery? Jesus, you are really into this, aren't you, friend? That's Maria's area of expertise, you know. By last count, she has three walls covered with floor-to-ceiling shelves of mystery detective thrillers. To your point: who would kill Farleigh O'Brien? Well, I could name several. Including the two of us. God, how I envy you."

"But we, you and I, we don't have a motive for killing. For tar-and-feathering, for castrating, for releasing condors to pick at his liver throughout eternity, yes yes yes. But killing?"

"Let me get back to you on that. Perhaps at the gravesite, swimming upstream against the Niagara of tears, seeing...no, hearing...the forty-seven elegies, I might be lifted to heights of new awareness. I guarantee you we will be hearing selections from Milton and Whitman. I bet you four thousand five hundred seventeen dollars and twenty-three cents someone reads 'Lycidas.' Maybe even Houseman. 'To An Athlete Dying Young.'"

"Jesus, I'd like to talk to you about what I'm doing here. I mean, trying to do. But I don't want to come on campus to do it. And we won't be able to talk in the car."

"The ladies are with us, bless them all. Maria's and Emerald's lowercase god has died. How about Sunday morning? Come for breakfast. While they weep, you and I can meander through the woods pretending we're looking for mushrooms."

"Done. Bagels and lox and cream cheese. For me, not for Emerald. She'll have a lettuce leaf and a grape. She'll probably still be wearing black."

"Maria, *aussi*. I have throughout our marriage of a hundred and twenty years given her credit for sensitivity and intelligence, but I'm going to have to reconsider. You know, if that so-called man had gone on living he could have had three different virgins in every vestal. What was his secret? Do you come up with secret strengths in this novel you're so into, man, like I mean, whatever?"

"Farleigh O'Brien was a po-et, Professor Scarborough. In your and my circles po-ets have more allure than quarter-half-fullbacks."

"Wouldn't trade twenty major po-ets for a single Brett Favre. See you tomorrow, friend. I'll drive."

❧

Forest has never read, let alone written, a thriller. Is a thriller synonymous with a mystery? A detective story? Must a thriller or a mystery contain a detective?

What are the rules here? And who are the rulemakers?

61

Should he read a couple...let's call them mysteries, since he is emotionally incapable of writing
thrillers and too ignorant of real life to write a detective story. Should he read a couple mysteries to get a
sense of the terrain? He will talk to Maria Scarborough
at Sunday morning's breakfast. He will request a few
recommendations of authors and titles.

But perhaps he should stay clear of the terrain,
perhaps he should stay clean. Not be led into temptation to imitate. Could his innocence produce a genre
of its own? A combination detective-thriller-mystery
novel that is also high-cult lit? Here comes Maugham's
dictum about there being four rules for the writing of
great fiction but no one knowing what they are. Just
write, Forest.

Just keep writing the damn thing, Forest. Worry
about what it is after it is. And remember, Forest—Sunday
morning breakfast will be mere hours after Saturday's burial ceremonies, so neither Maria nor Emerald will be able to speak a word through their tears
and rending of clothes.

At dinner, when Forest mentions the Sunday
morning invitation, Emerald shakes her head. She
will stay home.

"You and Paul continue your poster-mortem on
Farreigh at the table. Maria and I wash dishes. We
come home you sit at computer. I go shop for dinner."

Not a moment of pause to try to correct errors.

"You go to breakfast arone with Paul. I want to
meet Maria we make our own prans. After funerarl,
Saturday, we go dinner to restaurant?"

"My, my. *Quel hostilite.* I must say, Emmy, you've
been in a nasty mood for months. What is it? Have I
committed some unpardonable crime I'm not aware
of?"

Emerald, considering the accusation, too obviously judging herself guilty, glances away, starts for the kitchen, then returns to embrace Forest.

"I am velry, velry sorry," she says. "We go Paul Maria's house you sit at table you and Paul have contest. Arlways."

"Contest? We arm-wrestle? I bet Paul I can hold my breath longer than he can?"

"You try see who can be meaner, you try see who make funnier joke about Farey. This makes me hurt, makes Maria hurt. We hurt for you and we hurt for Paul and we hurt for Farey. And we hurt for us."

She is more correct than she knows.

Very well, he will try to get the message to Paul. *Let's go easy on this Farleigh O'Brien crap, Paul. Let's talk about classes, Paul. Let's talk about books, Paul. Politics. You going to vote for that Proposition for Gay marriage rights? Lets talk mystery novels, Paul.*

Paul will hear him out and then pretend to choke, and when he thinks Maria and Emmy cannot see him, he will assign the shame-sign, aiming one long finger at Forest and rubbing it with the other long finger.

Emmy and Maria love to talk about fashion. They are constantly showing each other articles or photographs from newspapers and magazines about shoes or dresses or hats or jewelry. What Julia Roberts or Paula Abdul or Fuzzy Wuzzy wore on the red carpet at the Oscars.

They will escape to Maria's room, where they will talk of...whatever it is they talk about these days. Actually, thanks to Emmy's trust and honesty, Forest knows what Maria and Emmy talk about these days.

"Tell me, love. What is it that draws you and Maria to each other? How is it that you rely on each other so strongly? What do you talk about?"

He had asked this question some months ago.

Emmy, that night: "Oh, this is a secret."

63

"A secret?"

"Yes. Like Maria says—me to know, you to find out."

"Do you talk about your husbands?"

Silence. Then, on Emmy's face, an expression part surprise, part anxiety.

"Sex? Do you two campus wives talk naked sex?"

"Same on you. You are dirty old man. None of your business what we talk about. No, we not talk about sex. We talk about fucking and not fucking."

"I am shocked. Shocked, I tell you. You were a virgin when we met, but you are so blasé and informed now. You sound like a veteran lover."

Emerald, troubled at both her disclosures and the meaning of the word blasé: "I not a veteran. I want to be sailor, but Japanese Navy says no. I love the ocean. Moon on big waves, warm sand beach. But I do not like to swim in ocean with shark or walluses."

"Walluses?"

"Big seals, two long teeth."

"Walruses."

"Yes, walluses. I do not like to swim with shark or walluses."

"My love, you are a natural-born poet."

That moment, that night, Emmy began to weep. "Not poet. No. Farey is poet. Famous, famous poet. World crass poet. Maria say this. I say this."

That was then, months ago. This is now. Tonight.

Forest holds his beloved wife, rocks her in his arms. He so loves her loss of skill with the language whenever she is trapped in heavy emotions, when a movie or a television program or even the appearance on a page of the name Mishima sends her into raptures of breathless swooning. He is tempted to bait her, to force her to stumble over an enemy vowel or consonant. He rocks her now so he can prove to himself and to her that he loves her even more today than he did a hundred years ago when she was that innocent beauty from Kyoto just arrived in California.

She returns his kisses. She very gently takes his hand and draws it up under her skirt and up under her panties, and she presses his fingers against what she knows to be his favorite spot to feel and sniff and kiss and then, sooner or later and usually sooner, to taste. To not just taste but to eat. To indulge himself in a meal that reduces him to human sashimi. The most atrocious of sins, she had informed him early in their marriage, must be forgiven after such love.

She grabs his fingers now and uses them so effectively she comes. With exclamations screamed aloud in melodic Japanese.

This—this extasis in extremis—this has not happened since the first night of their marriage.

So, all is well again. All bids...bodes...well again.

CHAPTER 5

Saturday morning.

Coffee and scones at the Scarboroughs' home.

Coffee and scones and gloom with a capitol G.

All four seat themselves in Paul's BMW in silence, Maria and Emmy in the rear, Forest in the front with Paul. Silence reigns for five full minutes during the ride to the college.

Paul Scarborough, trying finally, and in vain, for distraction: "Domini-can, Jesuit, Carmelite, Jelly Donut, they'll all attend the funeral to give their own imprimatur of holy sanction to Farleigh O'Brien's passage from this state of piss to their syndicated State of Bliss."

No sign of mood-change in front or back seat, though Forest gives it a weak little grin of a try.

Paul passes through the gates at the entrance of the campus parking lot and continues to the faculty parking area. As he swings the BMW into a parking space near enough to the arcade to protect them from the rain, Maria says, "Farleigh spent a third of his life in these buildings."

"More profitable," Paul murmurs, barely loud enough for Forest to hear, "than being a realtor who practices surgery after he marries Nancy Rockefeller."

Could the ladies have heard?

Emerald removes her dark glasses to wipe her eyes with a tissue.

"After prayers in chaperl we go cemetery. There wirl be mud."

"I forgot to bring boots," Maria says.

Emerald, voice catching, says, "I forget boots, too."

"We don't have to go— " Paul begins.

Maria stops him short. "We most certainly do."

"I go with Maria. You wait in car. You don't want to go."

She sounds, Forest thinks, as if she *hopes* we don't want to go. Why would she be so tortured? And why would he be so stricken with such high-tension melancholy at the vision of O'Brien's body being lowered into mud?

He guesses that Emerald, given the approaching and inevitable death of mother and father, must be suffering a sense of loss that he cannot imagine. He reaches back over the seat, touches her knee.

"We'll all go."

"Of course," Paul says. "Ah, there are the Spaniels. They'll probably insist on reading something from…What would you guess, Forest?"

Forest shakes his head. "Shakespeare? *Lear?*"

"Shakespeare, perhaps, but not *Lear*. I'm betting Henry Four. Hotspur."

"A sonnet. Not Shakespeare but contemporary. Stevens." Paul sings out, "Be thou the voice…"

"Hopkins. No." Forest, glancing up at the mirror, sees Maria glance at Emerald and hears her.

"The two dinosaurs who hate poetry obviously loved it once upon a time."

68

Paul: "We—if I may, Forest—we still love poetry. We still love poets. However, name one living poet, man or woman, who dares stand in the shade of Gerard Manley Hopkins."

"Or," Forest says, "Wallace Stevens."

"Two tickets to the Rams-Forty-niners game it's Hotspur," Paul says. "That's how Farleigh would see himself. Chivalric. Romantic."

Forest snickers. "I'm astonished to finally find the world-famous Professor Paul Scarborough's one blind spot. Hotspur is such a pho-neey."

"Well," Paul says. "So nu, as they say in French?"

"It's a bet."

"What are we betting?"

"It will or won't be Hotspur. I say yes, you say no."

"You got it. Two tickets."

Straight ahead: the athletic field, the quad, the library. To the east, on the hillside: faculty offices and classrooms. Beautiful.

The campus, Forest thinks, is beautiful. Indeed, it remains beautiful even during a funeral. And he realizes that he, too, has donated just about half of his life to this college.

Remember that first day? That first day, when he'd come on campus to be interviewed by Brother Linus, then the chair of the English Department. The morning had been clear and balmy. He'd thought then, he now recalls, that, yes, he could settle here; he could teach and study and write here, not ever to be overwhelmed by the publish-or-perish storms that batter English departments at Harvard, Princeton, Cornell.

"The freedom," he'd written to a friend, "will guarantee me twenty more years of life, all of it serene. I know me, I'm a friend of mine. Believe me, I'm no nut."

Whoever had been responsible for the presence of the college in this bucolic retreat had tried to marry the cultures of Spain and Ireland. All the buildings on campus, new as well as old, rely on Spanish Mission architecture of the Western padres: thick stucco-surfaced walls to give an impression of adobe, arched colonnades sheltering not cowled monks shuffling to vespers but student-pedestrians in Nikes and tanktops. Like Irish public houses, their red-tiled roofs slope into copper gutters that carry the gurgling winter runoff down onto lush green lawns thick with clover. Spanish-Irish: a bit of the auld sod topped with taco sauce.

Forest knows that, not too many years before he came here to teach, herds of cattle had shared the land with walnut orchards. The cattle remained for several years after the walnut trees had been downed, but the bellowing of the beasts distracted students from concentrating on Saint Augustine's apologias for his sexual obsessions; and so, ten years ago, the animals were magically transformed into white-wrapped steaks for local markets. Saint Catherine's students, showing their registration cards at the local Safeway, still rated a 15% discount on the purchase of ground beef.

On summer evenings, when only minutes remain before the sun's disappearance, the giant cross (of brass, a fool's gold) atop the chapel's dome rises into the sky like a naked Renoir model upright in her bath beckoning all comers, male or female. Most of the time, in the rain or fog, mornings as well as evenings, the cross/naked-model remains invisible. In the fall, at dawn or dusk, when the rays of the sun slant at the precise angle, the cross/naked-model calls out to the pilgrims returning from their San Francisco offices, speeding along the neighboring asphalt highway to towns named Walnut Valley and Pleasant Gardens and Orchid and Sunlight Haven.

At the chapel entry, Brother President, referred to as Brother Roderick in ordinary exchange, face and thick hair cream-white, stands ramrod-straight to the height of six feet less six inches in his rust-toned Paulist Brothers robes. Were he bearded and sandaled, he would be a model for a toy reincarnation, with those miniature arms outstretched, palms pierced with carpet tacks. A *piccolo* Jesus succoring the suffering multitudes.

Brother President greets Emerald and Maria in hushed tones, a cover for his uncanny ability to forget names as soon as he hears them, especially names of women. No risk involved, he greets Paul and Forest as Professor Scarborough and Professor Butler. The women by gender.

"Thank you for taking time from your sabbatical, Professor Butler. Professor Scarborough. My dear women, we share this grief. We weep, all of us. Such a loss. To his family, to the English department, to the college, to the world."

Paul, off-camera to Forest as they step inside: "To the college, to the world, to the galaxy, to the universe, to Jupiter, to Pluvius, to Pluto. And to Uranus, Forest?"

The chapel, as chapels go ("And most of them are going," Paul, at least twice a month, reminds Forest) is an impressive contemporary miniature of a miscellaneous Gothic model, a collection of mahogany benches and tiled floors and high stained glass windows and dramatic lighting and organ music glorifying the promise of an eventual appearance by God. The program indicates that Father Thomas Scanlon will be saying the Funeral Mass.

But the Dominican priest is not yet present. He will probably follow the salutation by the still-absent quartet. When Father Thomas does appear there will be no missing him, his three hundred pounds

71

swathed in white linen and red velvet; and his basso profundo will shame the organ into silence.

After the mass, Father Thomas, an undergraduate classmate of O'Brien's at Santa Clara and current Director of Religious Studies here at Saint Catherine's, has agreed to participate in the public portion of the eulogies. Paul cites, in a whisper into Forest's left ear, five phrases of what, he predicts, will be a baker's-dozen polished especially for this occasion.

"My former classmate, beloved faculty member, poet, literary critic, philosopher of international stature. Twelve more on hold. How many in a baker's dozen, Forest? I forget."

During the semester, Father Scanlon is available to the students for counseling, to the Brothers for, as Brother President describes it, saintly guidance and is responsible generally to the campus-at-large for weddings, funerals, christenings and wine purchases. He rarely performs any of the high masses, but when he does he demands rigorous adherence to pontifical utterance and continuing loyalty to Latin liturgy "no matter how they operate in the hinterlands."

Father Scanlon himself admits that he is fast forgetting what he refers to as "the mother tongue," thanks to his obsession with the language of "his boys." These are a mongrel collection of rowdy Italian and Irish student-louts (methodically learning the fine art of how to be adult louts) who make up the rugby squad. Rugby is the one sport Father Scanlon had attempted during his undergraduate days, without success, as a student-brother at Notre Dame. Recently, he had informed a reporter from the Oakland Diocese newspaper, *The Catholic Call*, that in his time, he had performed all tasks required by the church except shoeing the horses.

Forest considers the man harmless. In fact, there is an unpretentious, almost prepubescent innocence about him that is close to endearing.

Not innocence, Paul Scarborough maintains, but another three-syllable term: ignorance. Paul assures Forest that the fumes of Father Scanlon's arrogant ignorance so infuse the quality of the holy water as to guarantee gastrointestinal malfunction and pulmonary infarction in every innocent little victim of his baptism ritual. The two Jesuit priests on campus, who perform the rites of the church and also teach in the religious studies program, consider the Dominican priest personally responsible for the Spanish Inquisition. Thanks to him and his ancient Dominican lineage, the shade of history that seems to forever cloud the Church's reputation for Christian love will never soothe the doubts of Protestants, Jews and Muslims.

The Inquisition? That was the Church's My Lai.

⤳

The reverberations of organ music work dust and rumblings out of every ledge and cornice of every wall and ceiling crease. On the dais, blessed by a caressing luminescence from a concealed single pink-tinged spotlight overhead, the naked casket floats on a pond of funeral flowers.

Paul's whisper: "Mr. Cleopatra's barge anchored in the Bile."

Not far from the casket and masses of flowers, four empty black chairs wait like slightly ill-at-ease guests that have removed themselves from the asthmatic swells and falls of organ music. The seats of two chairs hold polished violins, one holds a viola. A cello, a caramel-colored ghost, leans with sullen patience against the fourth chair. Before each chair, at attention, a brass music stand, like a well-trained servant, open hands containing pages.

"So beautiful," Maria whispers as the organ swells.

Paul Scarborough leans across Emerald's lap to question Forest, "Do I hear Honus Wagner's God-damntheherringrun?"

"Beautifurl," Emerald barely manages.

"Hey," Paul whispers too loudly, "put stained glass windows in any redneck bar in Richmond, pipe in organ music, and you could mount the next Debutants' Cotillion in the men's pissoir."

A woman directly in front turns to try to scorch him with a glance. Paul does not win her over with his slow sly wink and twitchy grin and, in follow-up, the small-child wave of his right five fingers.

Paulist Brothers and lay faculty members (and their wives) fill the first six rows. Just about all of the faculty (full, part-time, temporary, tenured) and more than half of the student body fill the grand chamber, white plaster wall to white plaster wall, back to the entry and outside, across the tiled walkway onto the parking lot where the hearse, Zeus's chariot, waits for the darling of the gods.

The now approximately seven hundred mourners include writers and poets and appreciative syco-phants from Berkeley and San Francisco, colleagues from Saint Catherine's, many tearful former and current students, assorted relatives. And Farleigh's former wife and daughter.

Bonnie O'Brien. No. No longer O'Brien. She had reclaimed her maiden name some years ago. She is Bonnie MacNeil again. Bonnie MacNeil, sheathed in black linen, looks radiant. Could she have mistaken this burial for a birth? Her tanned skin refuses intimidation by mourning's colors. The heavy-lidded blue eyes appear to be a lighter and brighter blue than Forest remembers. Lovelier than ever, thanks perhaps to the eye-liner, the blush, the dark hair not fashionably fluffed and curled but pulled back into a loose and somewhat disordered ballerina's chignon.

Dylanna, their daughter, recipient of her mother's blue eyes and generous mouth and the strong white teeth of her father, has given up trying to manage an absolutely rebellious burst of red hair. Dylanna: gorgeous youthful Medusa with swirling flames in place of snakes.

Three men and a woman, all of them solemn, all in formal black attire, glide on noiseless feet from the wings of the chapel's stage to positions in the dark oak chairs. The instruments surrender to all eight arms like lovers about to yield to long-suppressed desires.

Forest, glancing around the packed chapel, is not prepared for a sudden but solid swoop of sorrow. What could have drawn this many, especially the students, to express such serious condolence? Farleigh could not have worked with half, a third, a fifth, of those present. But here they are. Is it mere curiosity? Is it to pay respects? Has—had—Professor-Poet Farleigh O'Brien somehow established within the consciences of these students a faith in the soul's concession to hovering omnipotent angels?

And then the music that soothes every savage breast. Music. Not the noise but the music.

Listen to the beauty that is almost visible as a solid substance.

Forest, in his three hundred years of life, has had to struggle very, very hard to finally learn to appreciate a narrow splinter of classical music. It was much like learning a lost foreign language. Weaned from eclecticism by a one-time colleague who recently died of AIDs, he has been drawn, after an almost fatal bout with Tchaikovsky and other Romantics, to the Baroque. Italian opera, for some unexplainable reason he has no will to investigate, always gives him a soft thrill, like a timid soft-shelled semi-orgasm. Mozart and

Haydn chamber music provide an almost unbearable sorrow that is like the after-effects of one more hit of marijuana. (Which, as a graduate student, Forest tried for one semester when a doctor's daughter wooed him with a spaghetti sauce that was a mix of grass and catsup.)

Forest has no reason to suspect (but he does) that Emerald appreciates the music he chooses to play on his sound system not because she loves the music but because she loves him.

But why this specific music at this specific funeral? Does anyone here, other than Bonnie, know of O'Brien's ignorance of music (proven by his pompous scorn for rhythm in his poetry)? Have only Professors Scarborough and Butler learned that O'Brien's musical terms and musicians' names and musical phrases were lifted from the *Encyclopedia of Music* but, in line after line, offered as his own creation?

Forest thinks he must remind himself to, at the first opportunity, ask Paul why there must always be music at a funeral of an artist or an intellectual? And when there is music, why must it always be a cello and almost always something by Haydn? Why not jugglers? Or tightrope walkers without nets? He, Forest Butler, will immediately, on arriving home today, add a sentence to his will demanding trapeze artists and music from *Oklahoma* or *Carousel* at his funeral. No! He will request music from *Finian's Rainbow*, the first and best of all those high-kicking musical comedies. It's that old devil moon. How are things in Glockamorra? On that great come-and-get-it day. If this isn't love. Look, look, look to the rainbow...

But listen now. Listen as the quartet, huddled on their isolated spread of tiled floor like an assemblage of MacBeth's witches, plays Haydn, and as the two violins and the viola, having no choice surrender to the cello. "The Emperor Waltz," and on cue, Forest sees and remembers the voice and face of Max Goldstein. Professor Max Goldstein.

Forest does not turn to search for Max in the audience for fear of finding him absent.

Last spring, Max Goldstein informed Forest, during the intermission at a recital in Hertz Hall at UC, that he can no longer listen to "The Emperor Waltz."

"Every time I hear it I hear nothing but 'Deutschland Uber Alles.' Don't the musicians hear it, too? They can't be Jews. If they are, they've been raped by their goddamn muses and they're saying, 'Thanks, ladies.'"

Three members of this quartet are somber men in dark suits, all apparently Catholics, given their facility with the process of genuflection. The fourth member, the cellist, a young dark-haired woman in a black dress, could be Jewish, perhaps Greek. An animated olive-skinned face, eyelashes and orbs so black they might have been burned into the tissue, not waves but vats of jet-black hair to the shoulders, to the hips. She sways at the waist as her bow dips and glides, sucking gorgeous despair out of the core of the gleaming instrument. Goldstein, were he here (and now an irresistible and a hasty glance at the gathering of faculty indicates he is not) would murmur, "Her cello weeps, she does not."

The music stops. The quartet rises from the chairs and, in virtual levitation, departs, their instruments deserted in post-coital exhaustion on the chair seats. Except the cello, which remains upright, tilted on its stand, still in authority but also still radiating despair. (A bit ripe, Forest, but keep that image and that language close. First chance after arriving home: into the file of *Murder by Metaphor*.)

Nothing is sacred. Right, Paul? Right, Forest.

Finally, demonstrating an actor's instinct for timing, from one of the side chambers, sliding out of the darkness between two tall concrete pillars like a mammoth bejeweled swan, a priest, white surplice appliqued with gold and scarlet.

Father Scanlon.

Father Scanlon reads the Gospel. His sermon, following, lauds the artistic passion of "...the man whose departing soul brings us together here today."

"Death for Farleigh O'Brien is not a departure but an arrival...The soul of Farleigh O'Brien is at this moment ascending to the heavens, returning to the God from whence it came...The Lord welcomes..."

While Emerald and Maria contribute to the sobbing, Forest reaches to take Emerald's fingers and her body (her hands are engaged in carrying her handkerchief to her eyes) falls against his. This, Forest realizes, is true sorrow racking his beloved's body. His Emerald could not be more desolate were the funeral ceremony dedicated to him, her husband, her love, her savior, her own Forest. A glance at Maria Scarborough reveals brimming eyes, tear-stained cheeks, a compassion Forest wishes he could experience himself.

When had Forest Butler last wept with such force about anything? One time—midnight, before he was married, in a motel in Des Moines, Iowa, when he'd banged his shin against the edge of a table. One time—at the age of six or seven he'd caught his fingers in a car door.

But to weep out of compassion? Had he ever?

Think, Forest. Try to remember. *My childhood.*

<hr>

Forest's childhood is radio.

People describing how other people—people like them (Momma, Poppa, Teddy, Rose Anne)—were starving, were begging for pennies. He, little Forest Butler, on the farm in Indiana, he had to save his pennies, sure. He had to wear patched clothes, sure.

He and Teddy and Rose Anne had to walk long miles to sell eggs and butter, sure. But starve? Never.

Forest grew up hearing neighbors lament the dreary life of those other Americans "back there," meaning the other side of the mountains, the other part of the country, "in the east." His brother Teddy, gone to war in far away Europe, had been wounded twice, had been awarded fancy medals for bravery, had returned safely. Rose Anne? No one ever knew what happened to Rose Anne. She just disappeared.

Disappeared?

Disappeared, yes.

After the war, his parents, no longer able to bear the hourly reminders of their lost daughter, fled to California; and Forest sped through childhood and into and out of adolescence and went to college and returned for his brother Teddy's funeral (car wreck... drunken driver...Teddy the drunken driver?)

Forest Butler was a grown man living in Berkeley, defending his doctoral dissertation, when his mother died then, two days later, his father.

Forest, to save himself, searches out the face of his friend Paul.

And he is saved.

Paul Scarborough's slit eyes and wicked grin brings Forest (stop being a sentimental old bastard, Forest) back to reality. Or is all this holy rigamarole getting to him? Does he envy this mammoth display of heaven-sent sorrow? If he were to die tomorrow, there might be, to support the distraught Emerald Hyashi Butler, a few friends. Paul and Maria, of course, probably Tony Coniglio, five or six former students, half a dozen colleagues including Max Goldstein, Mary Beth Lederberg and...and th-th-that's all, folks.

Back now, for self-preservation, to this magnificently funereal funeral.

With most of the anticipated audience present to commemorate the spirit of Farleigh O'Brien, there can be no denying the love, the regret, the sense of loss, the almost tangible, almost luminous spirit that has settled into the chapel of Saint Catherine's College. Why?

Why is this man, this poet, of such importance to anyone? Why, especially, is he important to these people present here to drown in lamentation? Paul and he and a small complement of other faculty members have held O'Brien in contempt, yes, but could they have—had they—could they have or had they missed something? Woods for trees?

O'Brien had developed in many students (apparently in the several hundred here) a respect for the written word, for literature, for education, for mystery, for dreams. What the hell else is a college for?

How many youthful souls, in a career two times the length of O'Brien's, had he, Forest Butler, lured away from the ubiquitous beer-busts and bonfire rallies and rap music and raves and all the other orgies of current cultural barbarism? He could count them on one finger.

He leans back in his chair. To his left, Paul Scarborough is shaking his head, muttering to his wife, his words clearly audible.

"You'd think it was Rudolph Valentino's funeral."

Forest admits to irritation. *Leave it alone, Paul. The bastard's dead.* But hasn't he, Forest Butler, aided and abetted Paul's cynicism? Isn't he now writing (well, beginning to write) a novel of revenge and exposure that will please Paul? How can he dare be critical of his oldest and dearest friend? Is it a new respect for the accomplishments, provoked by the magical mystery born here inside this chapel, of Farleigh O'Brien?

Or is it a recognition of something else he dreads? Is he finding a reason to convince himself the man, the career, the death, deserves no novel? If not deserved, he'd not have to write it. At least not the novel he is determined to write. Is he afraid to take the chance, after two novels rejected, of having a third scorned? Trying to convince himself to retreat now and...

No.

None of the above.

Pay attention. Consider what's happening here, Forest.

There is a process of almost inappropriate spontaneity following the prayer of petition, formulated by members of the congregation, and an even greater sound after the priest's final words: "Eternal rest grant unto Farleigh O'Brien, O Lord, and let the perpetual light shine upon him. May his soul and all the souls of the faithfully departed, through the mercy of God, rest in peace."

Voices.

Like little firecrackers popping on their common fuse, voices sputter from within the congregation, calling *Requiescat in pace*, each call propelling the next until there is a general hum, all voices joined into one harmonious final chorus of *Requiescat in pace*.

Then, as if by command, silence settles on the chapel. A silence lasting for almost a minute. Father Scanlon, who had left the dais, returns, departs once more and returns again, as if someone, perhaps he himself, had disrupted established cues.

Then, with a scrape of a chair, a tall, well-coifed, well-tailored man of thirty or thirty-five disengages from the audience and come forward slowly to the microphone. He holds a leather-bound volume in his hand.

"I'd like to read," he says into the microphone, voice trembling, "from 'The Lake Isle of Inisfree' by

William Butler Yeats. It was one of my brother's favorite poems. Yeats was one of his—well, his gods. I remember Farleigh, in high school, memorizing not just lines and stanzas but entire pages of Yeats. With heavy Irish brogue he used to recite those poems when we sat on the banks of a lake, fishing. I'll miss you, Farleigh."

Thomas Peter O'Brien begins to read but breaks down, tries to continue but finds it impossible. He closes the book and returns to his chair. People in his row stand to let him pass; some clasp his hand, some embrace him, all of them, including Thomas Peter, weep. Several other relatives follow. An aunt with a magnificent, probably stage-trained, diction and projection, takes up the reading, brings unexpected tears to Forest's eyes; and he hears an unexpected gasp at the end of the first stanza.

To his left. From Paul.

Forest hears the poem end here, on the floor, inside his head.

Then, not in their gowns but in somber suits and dresses, members of the faculty come forward to read. Ten of them—six men, four women. Donne and Blake and Eliot and Pound and Lowell and Stevens. The Spaniels read, in duet, from Ginsberg's *Howl.*

Paul's whisper: "Well, Forest, we both lost. Or did we both win?"

After Ginsberg and Bly and Gary Snyder, Forest loses count and track and interest. The Bly—from that prolonged impoverished period before he discovered it fashionable and profitable to play the role of a man, not just a man but a bespectacled, bevested, be-coifed male warrior. He who had never fired a gun in joy or anger or clenched a fist with malice afore- or after thought, or never shot in or pulled out an arrow or a bullet or even a thorn from a comrade's body. Warrior? The Greeks and the Apaches would have howled.

Is it true the word for contempt is the same in Greek as it is in the language of the Apache?

Neither Paul nor Forest weep. They do not even blink.

After the faculty and the last family member and friend has offered their tributes, students volunteer to continue the ceremony. Scattered among the audience, they converge, find their way into the aisles and congregate near the microphone. Each student in turn constructs the appropriately solemn stance and mood, looking—in their tinted glasses and mini-skirts and fashionable fresh-from-Milan oversized trousers and jackets—like a well-stuffed Greek chorus at reluctant rehearsal.

One tells a story about Farleigh's working with her through ten rewrites of a poem she'd sent off to a prestigious quarterly in Texas that is now considering publication. She reads the poem, dedicating it to Farleigh. It contains the themes and cadences of the very young and very simple—almost simplistic—O'Brien, a tribute to fields, to rivers, to surf and waters, to birds, to spring in the high Sierras. The ecological history of the universe in a twelve-line sonnet.

Other students use their turns to praise Farleigh's unselfish attention, his ready friendship, his unquestioning support no matter what their goals. All of this, rather than boring Forest, makes him uneasy, as if he is catching his own children in deep conspiratorial deceits about which, for various highly personal reasons, he can never confront them.

Leaning forward, he notices that Paul's eyes are closed. He is sleeping, or pretending to be sleeping, with that familiar sneer on his lips.

Bonnie MacNeil and her daughter sit in the front row. Poised. Controlled. Dylanna's hair is a luminous red halo. That extravagantly Gaelic face could only have been designed by a North Sea Botticelli.

83

Are they really such devoted observers? While fountains of sobs rise and fall here and there throughout the audience, Bonnie and her daughter, holding hands, stare into a space they share, a space impervious to invaders.

Forest reflects.

O'Brien was raised a Catholic. As a graduate student at Berkeley, he had compensated for his hundreds of unconfessed boyhood sins by finding solace in a daily and publicly confessed atheism. During the mid-sixties such rebellion was a common device available to individuals when they made their break with whatever others-than-ourselves they chose to fault for their personal failings. Formerly indulgent Blacks confessed scorn for white liberals; white liberals confessed to an inherited, perhaps even genetic, hatred of Blacks and Latinos and Asians. If they were men they confessed to hating women; if women, of hating men. Catholics confessed to sharing their parents' conceptions of Jews as Christ-killers; young Jews, thanks to their perception of Israel as a client of the US State Department, found reasons to hate near and distant biblical ancestors (including—especially—contemporary prophets called not Abraham and Isaac but Mom and Dad.)

Such confessions, purifying the karma, greased entry into "higher planes of knowing." Paul Scarborough's translation: "...higher piles of bullshit."

Farleigh O'Brien's Marxist posturings in graduate school had required not just outspoken contempt for the president of the college but for the president of the nation and, ultimately, for the pope. At college teach-ins and draft board sit-ins and protest be-ins, O'Brien's support for the Students for a Democratic Society and his contempt for capitalism and his devotion to socialism hung on him like an ill-fitting suit purchased blind at the local Good Will. His life: altar boy; novitiate with the Dominicans (Paul Scarborough's

84

"corporation that brought you the Inquisition in living color—blood red"); pink-faced virginal graduate of Saint Catherine's; rebellious and bearded Berkeley doctoral candidate whose incantatory poetry, spawned from an ungainly union of Brecht and Abbey Hoffman and Robinson Jeffers, portrayed career academics as firemen spraying piss on oil fires. Admired: Francois Mauriac and Graham Greene and Kazantzakis as well as, and at the same time, Fidel Castro. Farleigh saw himself in the image of Che Guevarra-as-balladeer.

He refused to cut his hair. He grew a beard—wisps of fuzz that would have been unruly had it moved beyond the wisp-and-fuzz stages. He wore a black beret and army fatigues and favored black stogies, though he never inhaled.

He would endanger his life, for the first time in his life, by traveling to Mexico and from there joining one of the Venceremos Brigades to chop sugar cane in Cuba. To guarantee a camaraderie with the Cuban masses, he decided to learn Spanish. He gave up after the seventh lesson from Estralita Ibañez, whom he had impregnated.

Having learned ethics with his catechism, he paid for her trip to Tiajuana ($45). Accepting money from a cousin, she paid for the abortion ($500). Her parents paid for her funeral (borrowing three thousand dollars from the same cousin-nephew.

After his return from Cuba, O'Brien went for days without washing his hands. He wanted the machete-born calluses—the first and last he would ever bear—to remain as long as possible. He wrote a poem—"Homage to Workers' Hands"—that was published in *Granma*, the Cuban Communist newspaper. An aging copy of the poem traveled from one to another of the several walls of his various graduate-school dorm rooms, like a revered war memento, until, husband and father, survivor of the Revolution that had committed suicide, well-shaved, suited and tied, Farleigh O'Brien was offered and quite humbly accepted a teaching job at Saint Catherine's.

He bought a small but expensively reproduced Modigliani print for his office wall. It was about then that he took to wearing the black Stetson and those lizard-skin cowboy boots. Oh, and a carved leather belt with a burnished silver buckle. Would anyone be deceived? Apparently, yes.

That was in the late 70s. With the Revolution not likely to be resuscitated, Farleigh O'Brien was, he promised both himself and others, merely biding his time. When the streets ordered him out again, tomorrow or the day after, he'd scorn the sanctimonious campus for the next generation of velveteen barricades.

But fickle fate fluttered forward. About five years after Farleigh's arrival at Saint Catherine's, Paul Scarborough commented—with no provocation apparently but without explanation certainly—on Farleigh O'Brien's possible career.

"Forest, if it were to the man's advantage to rejoin the faith he'd be a priest Monday and offer his ass to the bishop on Tuesday to guarantee a free trip to the Vatican on Wednesday. I predict that in ten years Che Guevara O'Brien will be back in the church consuming the wafer and wine in some gourmet chapel in Marin County or Big Sur or wherever the so-called Human Potential Movement finds it profitable to set up its spiritual schlock-shop. Once back in the church he'll bore it from within."

When Forest's chuckle, provoked by that memory of Paul's portrait of the great poet, crowds in through the grunts and groans of the organ, it brings a gasp from a weeping Emerald; and the chuckle quite neatly slides into a clearing-of-the-throat.

Lots of good usable stuff here, a hastily controlled Forest assures himself. Words, images, quotes, insights. It would certainly be bad taste to bring out his notebook and scribble in it while he sits twenty feet from the flower-bedecked casket. But he will have no trouble securing these memories, anchored now in a sacred little well of his mind, waiting to be lifted out the moment he returns home and picks his way to his computer.

Forest sees Emerald lift her glasses to dab with the white linen handkerchief at her swollen eyelids. She as well as Maria had been wise to have anticipated the need for their darkest Raybans. He shifts his leg to the right to make contact with her thigh. Her leg twitches, flees. For distraction, Forest, unlike Emerald, who is now gazing down at her hands folded in her lap, directs his attention to the arches of the college chapel.

This is a church, a mere church—barely a church. Certainly no cathedral. Consider Rouen and Chartres and Rome. Here, in the shadow of the city of Saint Francis of Assisi, presumptuous architects had persuaded an ambitious diocese to sell cathedral image to a gullible Catholic public yearning for Spanish mythology. The Virgin Mary, were she to bring her newborn babe here from the manger, would weep, and the innocent babe would vomit. Saint Catherine's has been the natural choice for final services for one of her own.

And Farleigh O'Brien is certainly one of her own. In the last few years, O'Brien's name and reputation have placed Saint Catherine's on the cultural map of the nation, to the left and the right of Mills and Reed and Stanford. Wooed by virtually every Ivy League college, offered a Christmas bag of benefits, including almost total freedom from teaching and sitting on committees, Farleigh had elected to remain here at tiny Saint Catherine's. His stated reasons: "I learned everything I know here" and "These students are endowed with California dreamin'" and "I couldn't ask for more stimulating colleagues." The truth: he hated the rigors of New York and New Haven winters, he loved the California mountains and seashore.

Paul had suggested a third reason: in the East, he would be exposed as a very small frog in a very large pond of other holier-and-brighter-than-thou poets and intellectuals.

An hour? Two hours? Two days? It has to have been a week.

But death, true to life, brings relief. The ceremony has to end before the body takes on airs.

Before the lid is drawn over the opening, every person in the chapel walks up to the dais, floating through the pink glow and the rich, sickening scent, past the casket, where one of the most renowned poets in America awaits his final greeting-and-farewell.

Bonnie and Emerald embrace, Emerald, but not Bonnie, weeping. Both Emerald and Forest, as do Maria and Paul Scarborough, shake the hands of seventeen-year-old Dylanna. When Forest sets his cheek against Bonnie's, she murmurs a restrained but husky "thank-you," accompanied by a Mona Lisa smile that for just a moment possesses a flick of near-flirtation. Into Forest's ear as their cheeks remain in touch: "I haven't seen you for a long time. Call me."

Forest tries not to read enticement into the message, but he has to admit to a slight knick of pleasure—or is it anticipation?—in the vicinity of the root of his penis. Shameless, presumptuous cock. With the dead husband's casket but a few feet away you, you mindless worm, become a snake in her grass.

Father Scanlon speaks privately to Bonnie MacNeil and next to Dylanna. People stand apart, then move in close. Some students are departing. Several Brothers are standing by, waiting for the opportunity to offer their condolences to the former wife of the honored deceased and her grieving child.

Outside, Emerald says she wishes to walk to the car through the rain. She wants to be washed, to be cleansed.

"I can understand that," Paul says.

Maria hangs back, her and Emerald's arms around each other's waists, as Forest and Paul draw up their shoulders against the growing storm.

The dinner at Francesco's in Berkeley is sober. Forest has several margaritas and stares at the linguini he'd ordered but cannot pull into his mouth. Paul tells a joke about a Polish intellectual and is the only one who laughs. Forest is not able to come up with a grin. Maria and Emerald shove their untouched salads aside.

"The Engrish Department," Emerald says, "all there to honor Farreigh?"

"Twelve out of fourteen isn't bad," Paul says. "Farleigh would have made it thirteen."

"Ten out of the twelve admired him," Maria says.

Paul signals the waiter. "That they did, that they did." He nudges Forest. "You're awfully quiet, old boy."

"His nover," Emerald says. "He thinks the funerar, how he writes about it in his nover."

"You're right," Forest says.

But she isn't right. He is thinking about poetry, and how and when he turned away from poetry, how and when his intense love of poetry had changed to intense contempt. How, for the last five years, he had refused to teach any course that required attention to poetry.

That is what he is thinking about. That and this: two faces and two voices that pop up like string puppets.

"What is the boy going to be?" the neighbor woman, Mrs. Hasenflu, asks his mother.

"Oh," his mother says, "he says he will be a poet. He writes and eats and lives poetry. My Forest is very sensitive, you know."

CHAPTER 6

Emerald elects to forego the breakfast at the Scarboroughs.

"You and Paul will continue your...the word? Word after death?...Coroner finds..."

"Chopped liver?"

Teeth clenched, tiny muscles tightened at the corners of her jaws, her eyes almost closed, knuckles of all fingers pulled into fists, Emerald manages, "You make jokes now?"

Okay, enough efforts at so-called wit. Save your sport for Paul, your fellow sportster.

"Sweetheart, I'm sorry. You mean autopsy? Post-mortem?"

"Post-mortem. You continue post-mortem on Farreigh at restaurant when we eat. You and Paul pray games with Farreigh's death. You go breakfast Paul arone. I want I meet Maria—Maria, Emerald make plans just women together."

"I promise I will be considerate, darling." Is the loss of Emerald's facility with the language an indication of her desperation or her anger or her frustration or her pain? "I must say, Emmy, you've been in a very blue funk of a mood for two or three months. Long before Farleigh O'Brien's death. You used to laugh when I played with words, when I made jokes. What is it? Have I committed some atrocity I'm not aware of? I can't remember in our fifteen years of marriage your brooding so heartily for so long. I know I think I'm being funny and you don't, but..."

Emerald, considering the accusation, must judge herself guilty. She glances away, starts for the kitchen, returns on the verge of tears, pulls Forest's arms around her shoulders.

"I'm sorry, Forrest." Her body is quivering as if she is suffering a chill. "Things do not go good right now. I'm de-depressed."

A burr drops into and down through Forest's chest. Over the years, Emerald, in the midst of a group of his peers, has learned how to deflect exposure of her confusion by smiling when the audience smiles or, only a fraction out of synch, laughing when they laugh. He knows his beautiful wife is neither dull nor stupid, but he also knows hers will forever remain what he considers to be the classic Japanese woman's mind and manner at work—quiet, undemonstrative, submissive in her marriage, overly courteous (by American standards,) a winsome and innocent smile camouflaging a host of constraints neither he nor any American man can possibly comprehend. A first-class specimen, Forest assures himself, of the inscrutable Oriental.

For the last several months (to himself now, for his own enjoyment of his own wit): unscrewdable.

Even when Emerald had established this new and current regulation—anything goes except penetration—she has continued to perform what she considers the wife's traditional duties—the arousal of her

master to sexual percussion, especially when master
least expects or even desires such arousal.

"Aren't going well with us, you mean?" He holds
her more tightly and hopes she will rush to reassure
him. She does.

"No, no, darring. At work. My parents. My fai-
yure as your wife."

"Emmy, quit the job. You don't have to work.
You certainly don't have to work at Breitbach. Failure as a wife? Oh, Emmy dearest, you are perfect. I
don't deserve such a perfect mate."

Only in moments of extreme affection, or concern, does Forest use the Americanism, the diminu-
tive *Emmy*. Often it is Em, usually it is Emerald.
From the first week, she has almost beamed at the
sound of *Emmy*. Confessing, one night—a guarantee
that she holds a separate and secret and very loving
place in her Forest's heart—that the word *Emmy*
makes her "tick-erule" all over. The American L will
forever snare her tongue. Her own name, Emerald,
becomes a back-of-the-throat Emerard. Five times,
perhaps seven or eight times, she has seriously discussed with Forest the complicated legal steps required to officially change her name to Emmy.

*Forest: "No. To me, you are a precious gem. An emer-
ald. If you must change your name it will have to be Dia-
mond. Or Sapphire. How about Lapis lazuli?"*

*She had laughed at that. "Dimind Hyashi. Sapphire
Hyashi. No, no, no."*

"A long time I do not give to you now when you
are horny. I am not a good wife, Forest."

"Dearest Emmy, believe me, I sometimes believe
you so beautiful, so much a goddess, it is honestly a
sin to defile such beauty with my wretched tool."

"Wretched too?"

"Now, what's this about your parents?"

Rather than release him, she clings to him more tightly. "I receive a letter two weeks ago. Mother, she is very ill."

"Why didn't you tell me? Do you want to go to Kyoto? I will be terribly lonely, but if you wish to go, you must. I'm very sorry. Should I go with you? I could explore Japan. Especially Kyoto. I'd never be the ugly American, I'd be polite and soft-spoken. I'd not embarrass you.

"I feel very guilty sometimes knowing how much you've surrendered, coming here, adapting to America, to me, and I've never been closer to Japan than Puget Sound. Would you like to bring them—your mother and father—to Berkeley? They would probably be very happy here with you, and you could quit your job and give them as much joy as you give me. Well, almost as much. I'd still want the balance to tip slightly toward me."

She begins to weep. "You are such a kind man, such a good husband. I do not deserve you."

"Oh, shush. In fact, shushi. Now what would you like to do?"

"I call home tonight. Perhaps she feel better." She is the innocent young Emerald as she nuzzles his ear. "We go to Kyoto in the summer. In the summer everything is green. Even the air is green. In the moss gardens the green drips down. On the temple slopes the pine trees are dark green. Bamboo, white bark green-blue in the sunlight and shade.

"I like California because it is like Kyoto in the summer. I remember hot summer nights I suck ice cubes, my mother and father and I sit so cool beneath the wind chimes. My sister and I go to shops, and we eat very long thin white noodles served over ice." She sighs, shivers beneath the memories. "Now, we shower and dress. I go with you to the Scarboroughs."

Her kiss is that special code kiss, with just the appropriate gap between the lips to permit the tap of the tip of the tongue. A code that always signals: fuck me, fuck me now. Her hand brushes his trousers, pauses at his fly. She draws his hand inside her robe to press it against her so aptly named mound of Venus, his very favorite spot to feel and sniff and kiss and then, sooner or later and usually sooner, to chew. To eat. To devote himself to an elaborate meal that reduces both of them to human sashimi.

The most atrocious sins can be forgiven after such love. Perhaps this morning will be the end of the drought. Three months of denial could be considered not a sin but a minor plague. Perhaps she will let him enter her this morning. Perhaps she is suggesting, promising, a return to their pattern of so many years.

Unfortunately, the drought continues, though he accepts her now-normal mouthful of gifts, after which she directs his thumb, only his thumb, to the precise latitude and longitude of her own clitoral geography. She weeps and then sleeps in his arms. This has not happened since the first night of their marriage.

Twice he awakens, partially, to find her still sheltered in his arms. She smells of some perfume her sister sent her from Japan. Forest abandons himself in swooning submission to the scent.

She wakens when the phone rings, catches him in thrall to her perfume.

"Exotic frower," she coos. "Very expensive. In Japan it is knowed...known...in tenth century. Aph–Afro...Afrodisacks."

Then, out of the bed, she runs to the phone.

Paul Scarborough asks a yawning Emerald if the old man has forgotten they are scheduled to have breakfast together.

"We reave fifteen minutes," Emerald says. "We be your house twenty minutes."

Back to her Forest, she slides her body across his, gazing down upon him as she moves, brushing his face first with her thick black hair and then...slowly, tantalizingly...with left nipple, right nipple. When Forest groans and reaches, she giggles and twists free of his hands.

She rushes to the bathroom, calling, "Fourteen minutes we reave."

⤳

The breakfast begins with at least a promise of decorum.

During the meal, whenever there is even the slightest drift toward the mention of Farleigh O'Brien, Maria brings out more bagels, a new and different jam, fresh slices of lox, extra dollops of double-whipped cream cheese. Or she forces the focus, and her praises, onto *Silence of the Lambs*.

Silence of the Lambs. What a perfect and perfectly evil film. In spite of its dangerous consequences for women—would it drive young men now on the edge of depravity over the edge into copy-cat cannibalism? In spite of that fear, the film had kept her in its grip.

"Camera. Acting. Dialogue. Direction. Editing. Perfect. A perfect film. I was unsettled, apprehensive, for the whole two hours, but I simply could not deny its gift. I was horrified to discover I didn't want to escape. I cheered, prayed for the FBI woman agent because Jody Foster demanded that from me. Jody Foster: Miss-Perfect-Jawline of nineteen-ninety."

Forest is, more than ever before, impressed.

A year ago, two years ago, during a discussion about the Feminist Issue, Paul used Maria's defeats in her attempts to continue her work toward her PhD as an illustration of how even a tough and qualified woman can be defeated.

"She could have been the best," Paul said, "if she'd continued fighting. If she'd gotten her fid."

Maria's considering the film a work of art deserves consideration.

Maria, savoring the rare appreciation of her judgments in their midst, rushes in and on. And isn't Paul proud. And doesn't Paul, for some reason, have to pretend he isn't.

"I should tell you, Forest. For Maria, Spike Lee is up there with Demme."

"Come on," Forest says. "Spike Lee? Johnny One Note? Or rather, Spikey One Note?"

Maria moves in fast. "I think Lee's a genius. Nasty, dangerous, aggravating, but a contemporary genius. He's a fighter who can punch as well as box."

Paul compliments Maria for her use of serial metaphors but especially for using as a source of metaphor a sport she so detests.

Paul Scarborough—the infamous cynic, the scourge of emotional excess, the high priest of intellectual isolationism—Paul Scarborough is currying favor. Usually, even with Maria, Paul is above respect for the democratic right of opposition or difference of opinion. Why is he so accepting, so placid this morning?

Look at him, beaming like a father whose young daughter, having already proven her talent in calculus and physics, has just announced her intention to become an astronaut.

But instead of being disillusioned with Paul, Forest finds himself resentful of Maria's performance. How dare she even think of trying to dethrone the King Cynic, her husband. Where and how is Spike Lee nasty, he asks. Where dangerous?

"Describe a scene where he boxes, a scene where he punches."

Even as he asks, he sees and hears himself in class: *You, you pert little blonde in the back row, you think you're such a whiz of a student? Prove your thesis. Cite evidence. Don't rely on a sentimental caviling feminism to legitimize your eyelid blinks and lip moues and guile-y promises of rewards.*

He wishes he could call back his irritation, his pompous questions.

Paul, remaining silent, lets Forest find his way through this thicket of his own unfortunate making as Maria takes him on.

Pleased with herself as she does, she cites, for several minutes, specific films, specific scenes, specific characters, specific dialogue, specific assaults, specific humane curtsies to tenderness. Forest, both hands up finally in the universal plea for pity, pleading for the blows to stop, finally pushes his chair back from the table.

"I surrender. In fact, I have to admit I've never seen a Spike Lee film. But I will now. Thanks to you."

Emerald stares at Maria, eyes alight, both hands near her face, ready to clap. She squeals her pleasure.

"Defeated," Forest concedes, wiping his brow and flinging mock sweat into the air. "I want to change the subject. I mean to cavil. To lick spittle. Please. I need to read some mysteries, Maria. Lots of them. Who are your favorite authors?"

Flattered at Forest's submission and his continuing deference, Maria chooses to be coy. "Me? Little old me? You want my opinions about cul-cha-cha-cha?"

Paul, revived, wags a long thin finger in her face. "He said nothing about literature."

"Oh. Right. He said mysteries. Beg your pardon, darling. How presumptuous of lil' ol' moi. Well, For-

98

est, it depends on your interests. Thrillers? Shrewd detective vs. almost-as-shrewd criminal mind? Simple murder mysteries? A wham-bammer like Hammer?"

"Hey," Paul said, nodding his approval, "that's good."

"Spillane owes it all to Hammett—where do you think he got the name?—and Chandler. Spillane could not get his whole foot into Hammett's one big toe. Anyway, why this sudden interest in what we peasants read? Or what this peasant reads?"

"Need you ask?" her husband, the man with the Halloween-Satan-grin, asks. He turns to Forest, nodding approval. "So you're going to do it as a murder mystery."

Maria gives a fine performance of a patient dropping into shock. "Forest, you're almost as disgusting...almost...as my husband. Forget it. Ask one of your creepy crawly graduate students for advice."

"Please, Maria. I've tried two novels but I've never thought about writing a crime story. Or a thriller or a whodunit. I don't even know the titles for the various categories. But this crime..."

Maria holds up her hand to stop the rush of plea-bargaining. "Crime? This *crime*? In my book and in the state of California suicide is not a crime."

Emerald: "And not Japan. In Japan suicide honorabr."

The ease with which he lies does not, strangely, disappoint Forest. In fact, the shape and context of his lies (meaning defense) does not let him reassure Maria he does know the difference between fact and fiction.

"The book will be a novel, a novel by definition is fiction."

Maria waits. "Though there will be a murder it will not be a mystery. Not for the writer or the reader."

She (and Emerald) wait.

"There will be logical and easily comprehensible reasons for every action taken by every character."

Maria and Emerald wait, attentive.

"Along the way, but especially at the end, no un-answered questions, no late revelations, no tricks, no surprises."

Maria and Emerald wait.

"It will be a not-unexpected suicide."

Then: "Seppuku privirege of nobirity. Rerigious. Emperors, miretary heroes, great artists—many find it honorabr way to end rife. Mishima performed sep-puku. To his forrowers Yukio Mishima is a god."

Though it is not necessary, Forest reminds the Scarboroughs of his wife's admiration for the Japanese author.

"Was Farleigh not a suicide?" Maria asks. When Paul begins to chide her for trying to solve real life murders as if they are all whodunits with a path of clues to be followed, she bristles. "Well, smartass, was Farleigh's death not—spelled n-o-t—a suicide? Has anyone...*any*one...said yes or no, this is or is not a suicide?"

Paul: "If it was or wasn't, there's no literary law against Forest's writing it as homicide *or* as suicide." In response to the expression on Emerald's face, he very softly explains, "Homicide means a person kill-ing another person."

Forest's chance to chuckle. Emerald knows very well what *homicide* means.

He risks a gentle intrusion. He speaks of writ-ers—not just writers but artists—who are honored in certain cultures more than plumbers or carpenters or janitors. Of cultures such as Japan's where, as Emer-ald knows, it is as natural to see Mishima as a god as it is to see the emperor as a son of the Sun.

Emerald: "TV, newspapers, everyone report death of Farreigh O'Brien suicide."

"But I'm writing a novel, Emmy. I'm not interested in facts, in what reporters report. I'm pretending. I'm making things up."

Paul holds up a right hand in warning. "Watch it, old friend. TV and Hollywood are not interested in facts. Nor is our exalted press. Nor our exaltant government. Nor historians, nor college administrators, nor poets. Okay, mostly nor poets."

Maria is shaking her head. "You're not pretending, Forest. You're lying. You're going to write a biography of Farleigh O'Brien, and you're going to say it's fiction. Why? So you can cut him up without being sued? Lies, lies, lies. Christ, maybe you and Paul should collaborate."

A slight wince apparent in Paul's face, as if that needle went deep. He shakes his head and tries to simplify the theory.

"All fiction has its own truth. If it's fine writing, the story could be truth. If the reader believes it, is so compelled by the writing to believe it truth, it is truth for that reader."

Maria, the righteous judge, makes her pronouncements from some lofty bench, as if her experience in such matters gives her the right to declare indictment and conviction.

"And if it destroys someone in the process?"

Paul, the smiling prisoner in the dock, defying the judge and educating her in the process: "If the truth of the novel destroys someone then whoever—whomever—it destroys has no choice but to yield."

Maria tries to interrupt but he rides over her.

"He—oh, yes, or she—has to accept his/her destruction. Especially if he/she is an artist. A painter or dancer or actress. Most especially if he/she is a poet. Being artists, they accept the laws, stated or unstated, of their art. They cannot be artists and believe in control, in censorship, in submission to popular opinion when the populace fawns over judgments made by frauds. Such people who submit to public opinion are politicians, not artists."

"More of the same academic bull pucky," Maria says. "What else is new? I have no idea what all that *perfesser* means and I doubt you do. You haven't enlightened me even though I've heard that spiel forty times. Now I know why I never got my Ph.D."

Her contempt appears to be directed as much at Forest as it is at Paul. Forest is puzzled. Is he sitting in on a daily segment of an ongoing family argument? The exchange surely has little to do with him and Emerald, or with him and his novel. Surely?

"If Maria won't," Paul says, "I can tell you some titles, Forest. I know the writers she admires."

"Don't you dare." Maria glares at him. "If this is going to be my show I'll do the performing. Okay. I have no idea what you're doing or why or how, Forest. But I suggest starting with Margery Allingham. Especially *Tiger in the Smoke*. Then her *Death of a Ghost* and *Black Plumes*. Josephine Tey—any of her books. And P. D. James. Take your pick. Try Paretsky's Warshawski books, if you can stand still for a bright, honest, strong woman. No Jane Austen, any of them, you'll say, but neither is Hemingway or Faulkner or Fitzgerald a—the—Ms. Jane Austen.

"For clever technique and skillful use of red herrings, the old reliable—Agatha Christie. And Sue Grafton, like Paretsky tough, sexy, decent. I fell in love with her Kinsey Milhone. I doubt you will.

"Ross Macdonald's *The Name is Archer* and/or *Sleeping Beauty*. For smart detective work, fine writing, Nicholas Freeling. *Love in Amsterdam* is about Holland but read any of his books. He has a good homey human detective. Or Janwillem van de Wetering. Also Dutch. Quirky, complicated, intelligent. *Blond Baboon* or *Butterfly Hunter*. That's just for starters. Enough?"

"Can I borrow your copies?"

"No, I don't lend my books. But I'll write the authors and titles down, and you can get them at the library. Or buy them and write off the cost. After all, it's research, isn't it?" She appears to be debating with herself whether to stop there or go on. Then she goes on. "You've decided not to have your hero, whatever his name is, commit suicide. Someone's going to kill the unfortunate poet. His wife? Thinking long-suffering Bonnie, Forest? A competitor? You, Forest? Paul? Another poet? A lover?"

Damn the woman! Her swift and apparently easily conceived concoction of the very questions that had been perplexing Forest for three days has come to her so easily, so rapidly. What the hell has she ever written to justify such creative felicity?

Emerald pours tea into her cup, then groans when she realizes she'd already filled it a moment before. She scurries to the kitchen for a sponge, asking, "What is the American expression? Ret the dead...?"

Paul starts to repeat the *ret* but thinks better of it, saying, "Let the dead bury the dead."

Forest laughs. "Emmy, you continually surprise me. Where'd you get that? And how's it fit in here?"

Emerald shrugs and offers the giggle that always wins over even her severest critics, of which, perhaps, there are two—her less beautiful and quite dreary older sister Michiko, still in Kyoto, and herself. She covers her mouth with her free hand but continues giggling behind the long slim fingers.

Forest, troubled, cannot deny the jab of self-incrimination in his heart. When he glances at Maria, hoping for sympathy at least, he finds himself returning to his own doubts about his own motivations.

"Tell me, Paul. In all confidence. You and I, are we motivated by envy? Are we envious of Farleigh's fame? Is...was...O'Brien really the best of his generation? Was he a contemporary Blake? A new Donne? A lot of critics you and I respect think so."

"Forest, Forest, Forest. Come on, Forest. If anything, O'Brien's not even warmed over or over-donne Blake. Anyway, what critic criticizes poetry anymore? Most so-called critics of so-called poetry are other so-called poets. Vendler's the only critic I read because she has no axes and knows more about the caverns of the mind and how they fill with song than any living poet. And many dead ones. I trust Vendler. She also happens to be an excellent writer. Her weakness: she treats poets as if they deserve attention, as if they are important.

"For the last century, poets have existed only to scrub each other's backs. You give my book a blurb, I'll give your book a blurb, you get me a high-paid reading, I'll get you a high-paid reading, you get me a grant, I'll get you a grant, you get me invited to this writers conference, I'll get you invited to that writer's conference. Do popes criticize previous popes? Do bishops complain about the cardinals? The code that poets swear allegiance to descends from the same code doctors swear allegiance to. Have you ever heard one doctor criticize another doctor in public? Or, especially, in court?"

"Emmy and Maria might have a point about our being..."

Paul sighs. "Envious? Look, Forest, don't turn drippy-droopy in your approaching old age. We knew Farleigh O'Brien. We watched him hypnotize our colleagues and students and audiences. We, you and I, knew the whole man. He was all intrigue and self—I hate the word—self-aggrandizement. A mouthful of coarse, unmanageable consonants and syllables. Like electronic music." A deep breath. "So, my friend, it's going to be a mystery novel."

"I think so. I had a call from Anthony Coniglio. Remember him? Very bright. Went into police work. He's moving up fast in—"

"Oh sure, I remember Coniglio. He's a detective in the city."

"That's him."

Emerald gazes at Forest over the rim of her teacup. Maria, setting her cup on its saucer and spilling tea onto the table, attacks the spreading pool with a handful of paper napkins.

"I remember him, too. A mucho macho guy in Armani."

"Anthony?" Emerald says. "We not heard from Anthony maybe three, four years. You cawed him? Why?"

He avoids answering her question by saying, "He called me. Anyway, he thinks it just might be murder. Can't say for sure, can't say who, but he has his suspicions."

"The papers haven't indicated anything but suicide," Maria says.

"Not really true." Forest speaks carefully. After all, he is speaking theory in front of an expert. "Everyone's been saying 'possible suicide.' But even if it was suicide, there's nothing wrong with my fictionalizing the story."

"That's what fiction is, ladies." Paul's voice begins to take on that slightly supercilious tone reserved for graduate students who assume themselves his equal. "True life made untrue but possible. With the very best writers, not just possible but probable. Peek into Joseph Conrad instead of Danielle Steele."

"You're drooling piggy pedagogy," Maria says. "What's the coroner's report say, Forest?"

"Nothing official yet. Tony is careful of what he says."

Maria touches Emerald's hand with the tip of a forefinger to catch her attention and then, to Emerald's delight, circles her ear with the tip of the free fore-finger, and murmurs, "Cuckoo, cuckoo."

Paul quite obviously does not approve of her nastiness. "That's what's beautiful about writing fiction, ladies. Forest's writing a novel. He can make up a coroner's report. He can make up the *coroner*. He can make up a coroner who, for whatever reason, lies. He could even make the coroner the killer. Maria, has anyone ever had a coroner as a...?"

Maria simply ignores him. Paul shrugs, as if he has been misunderstood, but he does permit himself a thin grin.

"You can't make the killer another poet," he says. "Poets can't kill. They can only rhapsodize about killing. Single exception: Wilfred Owen. He killed and wept about it but accepted it as his job. You the killer? Me?"

"No. That would be too obvious, too simple, too trite, too..."

"Predictable," Maria puts in. "You're learning."

"I have an appointment with Mary Beth Lederberg on Wednesday."

"Not my idea of a potential killer," Paul says. "Are you going to interview everyone in the department and put them all together into one?"

"I'm not sure. I need to interview three or four, definitely. People who've had long or intimate or nasty friendships with him. Or both. I'll start with Mary Beth and Max Goldstein. He's in the French department, but there are stories about him and O'Brien. I don't really look forward to socializing with many of our other colleagues. Not even Mary Beth or Max, who are the best of the batch."

"The best of a bad batch, me bucko. Why not make up your colleagues? Put a Spike Lee in there. We've hired a black guy for next year, so he's just naturally a suspect. Right? What about an Ezra

Pound type? A crypto-fascist who writes cryptic verse. Make him a born-again Coptic Christian, and he could write cryptic Coptic verse. But who the hell am I to advise you? You've written novels."

"Two, both rejected. After never having had a single article rejected by fifteen top journals in academia."

"My God," Maria says. "I see a glow of enlightenment and humility at the middle of the tunnel."

Paul gives Forest two thumbs-up. "Get on with the writing. Nothing about my thoughts you don't already know. You do know Mary Beth had a pretty intense fling with him?"

"Him? Farleigh? No, I didn't know."

"Intense but brief. About three years ago."

"She's gay," Maria says. "Come on, Paul."

"She wasn't gay then. At least not exclusively. Maybe..." With an appreciation of the novel idea. "... maybe he was the cause of her going lesbian."

Neither Maria nor Emerald seem impressed with the ramblings, humane or inhumane, of either husband. Maria is holding her head in both hands. Emerald is staring into her tea.

~⊱~

Forest, on the way home, reminds himself to incorporate all that exchange into his current notes. He cannot bear to even glance at Emerald, who is curled up into her seat, right cheek against the window. On such occasions, she has an uncanny ability to read his thoughts. Is she reading his thoughts now?

Okay, Forest, think scholar, think scholarship, think research.

How can a scholar betray anyone or anything? Scholarship, translated in any one of two hundred languages, means reliance on truth.

107

Scholars, by definition, are incapable of betraying.

Forest. Face it. How could you ever ever ever betray Emerald Hyashi Butler?

No.

No matter the temptation, no matter the possible opportunity, he will remain the objective researcher.

He looks at his wife and smiles. His wife does not smile back. She keeps her right cheek against the cool glass.

～⁑～

One message waits on his machine. "Forest, Tony here. Call me when you get in."

He waits until Emerald appears in the yard below to do with her iris bulbs whatever has to be done with iris bulbs in late summer or early autumn. Then, in his study, he dials and waits.

"Tony, this is—"

"Yo, Forest. Thanks for calling back. Would you mind our having a little talk—informal, so to speak? This evening or tomorrow morning? Off the record. Know what I mean?"

"Sure. Don't tell me you've solved the mystery of Farleigh's murder. Or is it suicide?"

"Nothing on that yet, Forest. We're still tracking various leads. That's what I called you about, actually. You've been away for three days, right?"

"Yeah, I was in Missouri, doing some research for my book."

"You spent most of each day at the Feinlow Library, and you stayed at the Hermitage Hotel in St. Louis Friday and Saturday and Sunday nights."

"Jesus Christ! You investigated me."

"Had to, Forest. I'd investigate my old man if I had to. I'd investigate my wife, my own mother, my sons. Anyway, I want you to know you're not a suspect."

"You're serious. Thanks a lot."

"Sure, I'm serious."

"But this means you've decided it was homicide. If you're looking for suspects you're not buying the suicide story."

"You got it. Hey, can you talk now? I mean now, on the phone?"

"Sure."

"Let's do it. Tell me about Mary Beth Lederberg and Professor Scarborough and Professor Max Goldstein. I never had Goldstein when I was there. Me and languages, you know. I hardly speak Italian. I had Professor Scarborough. Couldn't take him. I mean, I couldn't take the course. Gossip in the dorms: he could be a nasty sonofagun."

"Come on, Tony. Are you serious? You're checking those three out? Goldstein and Lederberg and Scarborough?"

"I'm serious, Forest, but if it makes you uncomfortable I'll come over to Berkeley and you and me can go out to Spengers for a fish dinner and we can talk. Would Emerald mind eating dinner alone on a Sunday night?"

"You want to talk *now?* Jesus, you're moving fast."

"What I want is some information about these three people. I'm guessing you'd be careful, not say what you think, if Emerald was sitting there. Am I right?"

"No, well, yeah, you're probably right. Okay. Now's the best time anyway. Starting tomorrow, I'm going to be so involved in my work I probably won't have free time for a month or two. What would you like to know? And do they know you're checking on them? If you were any other cop I'd refuse to do this, you know."

"I appreciate it, man. But it will speed things up. First of all, do they know I'm checking? They have to know. I've already talked to each of them. Just a couple minutes with Mary Beth Lederberg. She's really sick, man. Goldstein—I understand Goldstein's never hidden his hatred of Farleigh O'Brien. Can you talk to that?"

"I'd sure as hell like to know how you learned that so fast. Who else did you talk to? Forget that. I withdraw the question."

"Thanks, man."

"It's true. Well, true for the last few years, anyway. I don't know what happened between them. They're in different departments, never had much to do with each other. They use to be, well, collegial at least. But recently, in the Faculty Club, I've seen Max, if he was sitting at a table with colleagues, and Farleigh O'Brien came over to join them, I've seen Max get up and leave. I once saw him leave a dinner he'd not even started eating."

"And Professor Scarborough?"

"What about him? We are close friends, you know."

"I know. Bad blood between them? Him and O'Brien?"

"Paul has strong feelings about life and death and breakfast coffee. He doesn't reign his feelings in and he doesn't hide them. He says what he thinks, whether he's talking to the president or a student or his wife."

"Did he like O'Brien's work? His poetry and his other stuff, his criticism?"

"Paul has contempt for poets and poetry and every living human except his wife and Emerald and me. And sometimes I wonder about his wife and my wife. He gets along with his daughter. That's more than can be said about most fathers. But he's no killer. Angry, yes. Mean, yes. Killer, no."

"I had a poetry course from him, and man, I was in over my head. Me and Ronny Catalano were the only ones in the class weren't English majors. It

110

wasn't a writing-poetry course, it was...we read stuff by poets still living. Most of them, anyway. I dropped out the second week. Nothing rhymed in any poem we read."

"One-forty-six."

"One-forty-six what?"

"English one-forty-six. Contemporary Poetry. Paul hasn't taught that course or any other poetry course for years. But neither have I."

"I switched to Survey of American Lit. Mr. Spaniel."

"One-thirty-one."

"One-thirty-one?"

"American Lit."

"Oh yeah. I learned a lot from Spaniel, man. I mean it. Hey, he gave me a B-minus. Me? Literature? A B-minus? He liked O'Brien's poetry, if I remember right."

"He did, indeed. He still does. So does his wife."

"Amy. Professor Amy Spaniel. Scarborough told me he was in the army. Not Spaniel. I mean him, Scarborough. In Korea. The First Cavalry Division. Won a Purple Heart and a Silver Star. The Silver Star's given for gallantry in action. Showed me his ribbons and his medals. He was in the hospital for four months."

"You got more out of him in twenty minutes than I have in twenty years. Of course, I've not tried. We haven't exchanged more than ten or fifteen words about his war experiences. I didn't know he'd won a Purple Heart, for example."

"Two Purple Hearts."

"That means he was wounded twice?"

"That's right."

"The Silver Star. I can't remember how I learned that. Not from him. Maria, maybe. Maybe his daughter, Nina. God, she's proud of him. Things must have happened to Paul in Korea. He hated the Vietnam

111

war, but he hated the protesters, too. He refuses to see any war movie or documentary."

"He doesn't talk about his war experiences with you? His closest friend?"

Forest feels as if he has committed some act of incivility. Why would Tony want to insist on details about war? He, Forest, had missed both Korea and Vietnam.

"Paul hates violence more than I do. I'm frightened of it."

"Me, too, man. Anyway, yeah, he was in deep doo-doo over there in Korea, man. He didn't brag, but I sensed it must have been hell. Maybe that's why he's sort of weird. Anyway, what about Lederberg. She a good professor?"

"The best. Why?"

"Never met her. She's gay, ain't she?"

"Tony, for Christ sake. How'd you find that information? She's gay and she's very sick and she couldn't kill a mouse."

"Ah, you'd be surprised, Forest, who can kill mouses. I mean mice. Hey, this has been informative."

"Who the hell have you been talking to? In forty-eight hours you've found just about all the dirty linen in Saint Cate's English Department."

"It's clean linen, man. Hey, I'll get back to you. Now we don't have to keep Emerald out of our talk. I'll call you, pick up on my invitation to savor more of Emerald's food. Savor. How's that for a cop's vocabulary?"

"Tony?"

"Yeah?"

"Call me if you decide things, will you?"

"Decide things?"

"When you know if it's homicide or suicide."

"You got it, man. Later."

⁓

Forest sits at the computer for almost two hours, and in the end, when Emerald comes in from the garden, slamming doors, he knows they will be eating lunch very soon.

He goes back to the beginning of Chapter 1. That first sentence will never be changed. Maybe various other sentences in the rest of the pages will go through a jumble of verbal calisthenics but not the first sentence. He speaks it aloud.

"Who killed Clancy Cavanaugh? Not me, though I have to admit I'm not sorry he's dead."

CHAPTER 7

3/22/93

Two reasons I intend to complete my interviews in as
short a time as possible. One, I need information
(perhaps because I can't quite shake my infection of
academic research) before I can feel at ease tackling
the story. Two, I don't want to put off the writing
with the excuse that I feel uninformed. I know myself
too well. I could spend weeks, even months, "re-
searching" rather than writing.

I know, for purposes of this novel, that I must
choose someone to kill Farleigh O'Brien (whose
name I will change to Clancy Cavanaugh), someone
credible, meaning someone with a legitimate motive.
I could arbitrarily pick someone and lead the reader
through a series of events that satisfy, that convince,
so that at the end the reader will say, "I thought so."
Or "I'll be damned, so that's who did it. You fooled
me, Butler."

Do I place Farleigh/Clancy in a setting I know
very well, surrounded by a cast I know even better,
and write the novel fast, with the self-assurance I

need? Or do I place Farleigh/Clancy in an exotic environment, which I create but which is false (meaning unfamiliar) and stumble around with nagging apprehension for months or even years, feeling like a stranger in a strange land?

No, go for the familiar. I'm not inventive. I'm a creative plodder, I can put words together fast so I'll get this done fast. The next novel, if this one works, will be deeper, more demanding of both me and the reader.

Let's play scientist, let's deal with facts. Fact 1: I choose an English department at a small Catholic liberal arts college in California. Fact 2: From that English department, I select one person who does the killing for reasons I know but which I only permit the reader to discover along the way. (That, I've learned from reading six of the ten novels Maria Scarborough recommended, is the accepted pattern.) Of the thirteen members in the Department two or three will be suspect. It's important to keep the number at a minimum. Fact 3: Use Tony. Tony's list helps. It's crazy, obviously. Totally unreliable. I'm certain none of those three can kill.

But it's now my job to make someone (one of them?) possessed of whatever mix of social and literary hormones makes a killer. Tony's handed me my cast of characters on a police blotter. I'll interview the three to get necessary and more intimate information, details that will help me create complex but credible characters, a quality important in all fiction but especially in a murder mystery, if I want it to sell. (Meaning: be bought by a publisher.)

I'll start with Lederberg, then Max Goldstein. Finally Paul Scarborough, who, I predict, is delighted to be included among Tony's trio of desperadoes. His photograph on post office walls as one of the TEN MOST WANTED CRIMINALS would be more satisfying to Paul than winning the National Critics

Award. He's always had fantasies of being a sort of professorial Hell's Angel, riding into a department meeting and battering the eggheads sniffing at the heels of the latest scholarly fad. (Like those Deconstruction Terrorists at Saint Cate's and every other college in the country. A con-job.)

Oh, wasn't it sweet when the idol of those smug, smarmy, self-righteous pseudo-intellectual Vikings turned out to have been a Nazi!

"Blame the Germans now for being taken in by Hitler," Paul had screamed at O'Brien and Alvin Paley and the Spaniels and the younger part-time slugs who left their slime-trails on the floors of Saint Jude's Hall.

Can I find a place in the novel to get this Decon in? (Reminder: play on the word *Decon*, which is the name for a poison fed to mice and rats!)

Tony will keep me on-track. After all, whether it is or is not suicide is unimportant. If it turns out to be homicide, and the killer is some anonymous outsider—the cleaning lady, the postman, a student—I can ignore the reality of his/her word. I don't have to worry about truth. I'm not a philosopher. And what philosopher deals with truth anyway?

Wait a minute. Wait a frigging minute. What was that six or seven lines ago? A student. Have to think about that. Why *not* a student? Man or woman? No matter. Student it is! And Leslie's the lass. Change Leslie to Elizabeth? Cindy? Patty? No, Patti. Excellent. Patti. Patti Andersen. Patti Jane Andersen. Perfect.

THE INTERVIEWS

3/22/93

1. Mary Beth Lederberg

Mary Beth Lederberg. Bachelor's Degree University of Michigan, 1965; Ph.D. Princeton, 1970; faculties of Michigan and U.C. Berkeley 1971-1978; Saint Catherine's 1979-current. Special interest: Contemporary feminist literature.

My impressions of MBL before the interview.

Originally, when she came to Saint Cate's, I found her very attractive. She seemed quite feminine, exceptionally bright, concerned about adapting to the needs of a small English department in a small liberal arts college. Tenured Saint Cate's in '86.

About four years ago suddenly seemed to harden. She dressed differently, rarely used makeup and jewelry, no longer seemed to care about appearance. Has been ill for some months, struggling to attend classes. I have covered her classes four times, as has Paul Scarborough, as have other members of the department. She is considering taking medical leave next semester. I suspect cancer, though there has been no public announcement.

She continues to work hard at the college those rare days she's there, remains devoted to the students, demonstrates her affection for me readily, without restraint. Until this semester has been more than willing to accept her share of undesirable courses, committee work, unpleasant chores.

MBL's three books, published by an east coast feminist press, have been very significant contributions not just to feminist literature but to critical literature in general.

She and I have always treated each other with trust and respect. Differing sexual proclivities have never bothered either of us. There is a rumor that won't die that MBL came to lesbianism late, and that, in fact, she'd had a male lover as recently as seven or eight years ago. If Paul is to be believed, she had an affair with O'Brien three or four years ago.

Now forty-six years old, she lives with a slightly younger woman who is not involved in academic work. They have lived together for five years, are open and cheerful with each other whenever I have occasion to see them socially. Her companion, Jeanne, is shy, on the fringes of college activities, has always been friendly but guarded with me.

Mary Beth and Jeanne live in a cedar-shingle home on Stuart Avenue in Berkeley, a block east of College Avenue. Like her office, Mary Beth's home is clean, orderly, furnished in casual good taste, with an abundance of roses from their own garden, which Jeanne tends.

MBL is quite melancholy tonight. Not until now have I been aware of her weight loss. She appears ravaged by the cancer. To distract her visitors, or at least me, she is wearing very heavy makeup. It is so thick on her cheeks and neck as to be quite distracting, even a bit repulsive. It is as if she is trying to deceive herself as well as me.

Interview was conducted Monday night, March 22nd, 1993. I was invited for dinner. I thanked Mary Beth for seeing me on such short notice, and she said she wasn't sure yet whether she should be thanking me in return. Not yet, anyway. We talked campus and national politics during drinks and hors d'oeuvres and then from eight until nine we conducted the interview, which, with her permission, I taped and, without her permission, have edited. She was tired, or the interview might have gone on longer.

Following are only highlights relevant to *Murder by Metaphor*. Mary Beth does not know I will be writing a novel. I informed her, as I will inform Max Goldstein, that I am writing a book about Farleigh O'Brien. Being academics, knowing my interests and publications, they and everyone else will assume that by book I mean a critical study. I can't permit myself to worry about how I'll respond if and when this novel is published and they announce their resentment.

Forest Butler: Now, about Farleigh O'Brien. What were your reactions when you heard about Farleigh's death?

Mary Beth Lederberg: Tricky, Forest. You just take for granted that I, like you, distinguish between thinking and feeling. I know that you, as I do, always try to get your students to recognize that distinction.

You ask what my reactions were, leaving me to separate feelings from thoughts. Okay. Fair enough. First, what I felt. Shock, of course. Hopes that the story as reported might prove false. A sense of loss. He was so talented, so young. His best years were ahead of him. He was a remarkable poet and an even more remarkable essayist.

What I thought. I thought why did he kill himself? What were the problems that could drive such a person, a poet/scholar in his prime, to such an act?

Farleigh and I had been close at one time. At least, I thought we were. Now, I realize I didn't know him at all. I wonder if anyone did, including Bonnie.

I thought about what I learned from his poetry, his books, his critical articles, his readings, his performances in our department meetings, what critics and reviewers said about him. Nothing explains this, if *this* means suicide. How—and I'm thinking about this—how can I feel sad about someone I thought I knew and now discover I didn't know at all?

In truth, I guess I don't feel anything at all. Not sadness or remorse or revenge. Strike that. I'm too old and suddenly too mortal to think about revenge. When I think about Farleigh's death I ought to feel *something*, but I discover it's like trying to feel sympathy for a pebble that's been crushed.

FB: I remember a night Emerald and I were here. You and I had drunk a fair amount of wine. We took turns reading aloud. Auden, Lowell, Pound...

MBL: Bishop and Berryman. And Levertov and Sarton and Piercy and Adrienne Rich.

FB: O'Brien had just that day been awarded the Pulitzer Prize. You surprised me by being upset. Before the evening ended you scorned the praise and awards O'Brien had been receiving these past few years. You said he was a poseur. That was the first and only time I ever heard you be—

MBL: Nasty. I regret that. Let's blame the wine. He was unwise, impatient, took stupid chances, tried dishonesty, but especially in retrospect, he deserved his award.

FB: But you did say it. I remember thinking you were very angry. Not nasty, meaning abusive without reason, but *angry*. With, I guessed then, good reason.

MBL: Okay. But you cannot quote me. Is that understood? I trust you, Forest.

FB: I promise not to quote you.

MBL: O'Brien's essay on two of my idols, Bishop and Sarton. The essay in *Transposition*. He and his wife invited us—Jeanne and me—to dinner. Among other things, we talked about Bishop and Sarton and various other women poets, past and current.

I tried to change the subject—Jeanne's not interested in that stuff. It wasn't fair. Bonnie O'Brien understood. She tried to guide us into architecture and design. That was fine.

But Farleigh wouldn't have it. He wasn't really interested in architecture, though he often pretended to be.

[Jeanne puts in with: "He's the same way with plants and trees. He can name every damn flower, both common and Latin name. But you know? He never *smells* the flowers." Mary Beth beams, looks at me to be sure I appreciate Jeanne's intelligence and unassuming aesthetic instincts.]

A half hour or so after dinner, I announced that Jeanne had to get up early the next morning, and we left.

When the *Transposition* essay came out it was filled with comments I'd offered during that dinner. They were presented in the essay as if they were his own ideas. No attribution whatsoever. I felt as if I'd been raped. I wondered about his other essays.

I looked at his now-famous introduction to the famous—justifiably so—Baudelaire book *Fleur e Poesie du Mal*. Max Goldstein and I were discussing the introduction one day. I found myself sniping at it, doubting its integrity. I confided in Max, as I'm confiding now in you. Max took a month to track down some of Farleigh's so-called insights. Many—most—were so close to plagiarism I was shocked. Very creatively, elegantly, camouflaged ideas and phrases, even similes and metaphors, of other poets and scholars. World-class forgery.

He doesn't read or write French, but Max said his translations were impeccable. How did that happen? Max was tempted to try some literary detective work. Had Farleigh hired someone? A friend? A French graduate student at Berkeley? I convinced him to let it go. He agreed to say nothing. Why provoke a trial that requires so much time and energy and depression? No one profits from that. Our own satisfaction was all that was important to us. We had that aplenty.

After that, I talked to Farleigh only if I had to, at department or committee meetings. Apparently, he couldn't have cared less.

Jeanne: But he did call you—what?—two years ago? When you won the Krakower Award for Women Writers and the Rooms of Their Own. He invited you to dinner. And you accepted. I was mad.

MBL: You're correct. Why did I go? Well, I guess because I fully intended to confront him then and there, in the restaurant, in spite of Max's and my own promises to say nothing. I guess I hoped there would be some confession. At least an explanation. Maybe even an apology. I guess it was important to me that he reclaim his image.

He didn't. In retrospect I was not so much angry as...well, I felt sullied. So I now share dear Max's contempt and anger. Max, as you must know, has had his own near-brawl with Farleigh.

FB: I'll be interviewing Max, too. But, that night at the restaurant, was there even a slight awareness on Farleigh's part, even the slightest concession of how he used you?

MBL: No. He was...well, he was terrible.

Mary Beth seems about to cry. Jeanne comes to her side, embraces her, holds her, asks if she needs anything. Water? Coffee or brandy? Mary Beth offers a weak, grateful, loving smile and shakes her head.

FB: Terrible in what way, Mary Beth?

MBL: Just terrible. Let's leave it at that.

FB: You were surprised that he committed suicide.

MBL: Yes, I was.

FB: Could you believe that it was not suicide? I don't say did you, but could you?

MBL: Do you have information that justifies that question?

FB: No, not at all. I just found it—suicide—so unlikely for a person who wrote and talked so brilliantly about the beauties of life.

MBL: Oh, yes, indeed. Couldn't he talk beautifully and brilliantly, though? And charm? He could charm the horns off Satan.

FB: Well, he died of a gunshot wound. "Possible self-inflicted," the papers said.

MBL: I've been wondering if anyone else had noticed that. A possible self-inflicted wound.

FB: We should stop. You're tired. Thanks very much, Mary Beth.

MBL: Yes, I am tired. I don't envy you your task. But I hope you pick up where Max and I left off. I honestly do. I've finally decided it has to be done. Villains don't just exist in politics or movies. They live among us, they have to be exposed. Don't evade it, Forest.

3/22/93. Nothing about an affair with O'Brien. Should I have been blunt? Would she have denied it? I think the presence of Jeanne intimidated me. And how/why should I be the agent of additional pain.

One thing I've learned—Mary Beth Lederberg certainly has strong feelings about Farleigh O'Brien. Strong enough to kill? Of course not. Anyway, I think she's more concerned about her own life right now than O'Brien's death.

2. MAX GOLDSTEIN

3/23/93 Evening

Goldstein has an undergraduate degree from Princeton and a Masters and Ph.D. from Yale. He has been at St. Catherine's for thirty-two years. His main interest: French Renaissance literature. Has published many articles, six books, all of them receiving commendations, one of them nominated for the Critics Circle Award, another for the Prix Goncourt. The French woman he met during his graduate days in Paris (Collette, or Coco) has not aged gracefully. Nor, in truth, has Max. Very respected at St. Catherine's but considered somewhat old-fashioned now (his French *passé* says it better.) Even eccentric. In the last few years has had little to do with college affairs. Eats a bag lunch in his office.

He and his wife share a sedate, isolated life filled with music and literature. They live in Paris all summer every summer. Not a bad life, I'd say. Their children have gone their separate ways. "With great relief on both sides, probably," Paul Scarborough says.

One reason for interviewing Prof. Goldstein: his sudden and ongoing undisguised contempt for O'Brien has been attributed to the psychological and physical failings of old age. What one of the younger and most impolitic members of the department calls "oldtimer's disease." (That young twit's failing, Paul Scarborough suggests, is "juvenile dementia.") But rumors persist. Now, Tony has him on his suspect list. And Mary Beth talks about an apparently intense contempt if not hatred for Farleigh. Why?

This interview was conducted in Prof. Goldstein's study in his home in Montclair, in Oakland, because, again, I do not care to go on campus. Not yet. I'll be there soon enough. For now I want to remain as detached, as objective, as possible. As with Mary Beth's interview, material included here is edited to include only that which I consider relevant to M by M. A part, perhaps three or four pages, might be of little relevance but I need to ponder it before I cut it.

Forest Butler: Max, you were friendly with Farleigh, early on.

Max Goldstein: Correction—I was a colleague. Friendly? I hardly knew the man. We talked at some length two times. Both times about the possible translations of French street slang he'd come across. I wasn't too helpful. He'd picked up some Moroccan patois when he was living in Paris. A mix of French and Arabic. Not my area.

FB: I'm not breaking any confidences when I say that at a certain point something dramatic must have happened. Your animosity was suddenly quite apparent. You never tried to hide it. Everyone recognized it. Would you tell me what happened?

Max Goldstein: Oh, I don't think that's really important. The man's dead. *Il faut laisser les morts ensevelir les morts.* Privacy. His, I mean.

FB: I'd agree normally, but the man is—was—a figure of national reputation. To some extent, international. Such figures have no privacy. Common, ordinary people have a natural, unearned anonymity. A figure of national or international renown surrenders all rights to privacy. President Wilson's madness, Harding's affair with the chambermaid, Kennedy's affair with Monroe, Cocteau's homosexuality, Hoover's cross-dressing, Robert Lowell's manic-depression, Madame Somoza's shoe fetish—that's all public domain.

MG: If, as a professor, you smoked dope with your students fifteen years ago, as I hear you did, can the college discipline you? Do you have a right to privacy?

FB: You heard correctly. And I don't have a right. If I smoked dope with students even in that more permissive time I deserve whatever punishment I got or get. I knew what the rules of this college were when I became a professor. I had—have—no right to protest.

MG: We disagree. I'll tell you only what I consider appropriate.

FB: That's all I can ask. Okay, I've talked to several people in the English department, and there seems to be a not too sizable minority with, well, with what I'll describe as concealed disdain for Farleigh. Was there disdain, contempt, resentment in your break with him?

MG: Oh, I'd not say I held the man in contempt. He has been rightfully judged a genius. But, of course, the famous art forger von Meegren was also a genius, wasn't he? And I certainly didn't resent O'Brien. You use the word *concealed*. I was simply being well-mannered. *Il faut laver son linge sale en famille.*

FB: Do you know anything about his relationship with Mary Beth Lederberg?

MG: Relationship? You mean, *un liason*? If I did, I'd not discuss it with anyone.

FB: I don't mean sexual relationship. I mean their professional relationship. Like yourself, Mary Beth, once close to Farleigh, turned decidedly cool toward him, especially during this past year or so.

MG: You insist on seeing our relationship as close. It was never close. Mary Beth's relationship? I'd suggest you discuss that with Mary Beth, old man.

FB: Max, I'm trying to understand the guy. It's important for me to know why people reacted the way they did to Farleigh. Most of the people in my department stepped on each other's arches to be positioned to anoint him.

MG: Not everyone, Forest, not everyone. Certainly not you or Paul Scarborough. Or Mary Beth.

FB: About that translation you and Mary Beth checked out.

MG: She told you about that?

FB: Yes. You found reason to believe he'd plagiarized...

MG: What? What are you talking about?

FB: Mary Beth told me...

MG: My opinion, that's all.

FB: You didn't find material he'd ripped off?

MG: Find? In order to find you have to search. I never searched anything. Never considered him worthy of the time.

FB: Okay, one more question. You'll think this an odd one but consider it. Do you think Farleigh O'Brien could have killed himself?

MG: That *is* not an odd question. Francois Le Clere says, "There are no foolish questions, there are only foolish answers." How do I say this? Farleigh could have killed himself, but he would have had to stand in line.

FB: Of course, I won't quote you. That is, however, the sort of epigram you might include in a text on Voltaire. Can you think of any person who might have held such hostility for O'Brien that he could...

MG: He or she?

FB: Okay. That he or she could have...

MG: "Committed this dastardly crime?" You sound like you're writing a novel, not a critical treatise. Well, I could probably name a dozen suspect poets. Or poet-suspects. Similarly a dozen scholars. More than a dozen former friends in the anti-war movement.

Poets by definition are impassioned. They are constantly reflecting and judging the state of themselves as well as the state of their society. They are fiercely competitive with the word and each other. The chemical mix that produces explosions is more complex and more intensified when the poets involved are also professors.If words could kill, both professions would be decimated.

You'll note I have resisted infection by the Paul Scarborough virus. He maintains poets are closet intellectuals. I've heard him say that because poets are full of ambiguities and never have to prove their quote unquote, art, poets can pose as cerebral aesthetes. To my mind. an interesting but simplistic theory.

My daughter's a nurse. She hates surgeons. She says they're prima donnas. They have to be, if they want to be successful surgeons. She's not sure which comes first: preoccupation with self or the need to cut other people open. Scarborough asks: are poets poets because they're intellectual poseurs or are they intellectual poseurs because they're poets?

I think that's Paul Scarborough's one limitation as a critic. His refusal, his inability, his blindness, his provincialism, his lack of sensitivity regarding poets. Why does he hate poetry?

FB: *One* limitation? You just named five. Max, he doesn't hate poetry, he just hates poets. And only certain poets.

MG: He tells me he has successfully, for more than ten years, avoided teaching a course in poetry.

FB: For God's sake, Max, for more than ten years I've refused to buy a Mercedes Benz. That doesn't mean I hate cars. Or the Mercedes in particular.

MG: Poetry is not a commodity.

FB: You sound like a nineteenth-century aesthete. Today all art is a commodity. Unless you know some artist who's giving his away free.

MG: May I ask why you are writing this book? Why waste your time? Surely, you don't think O'Brien deserves the attention, say, that a Ginsberg or a Lowell or a Stafford deserves. Or a Seamus Heaney or a Brodsky.

FB: Two or three of those are dead. Of course, so is O'Brien. Why such hostility, Max? Not just toward me and Paul but toward Farleigh as well?

Max, at this point, sits up. I've been a bit impatient with him, a bit snippy. But I wasn't going to indulge

129

him. He had no right to put Paul down, even though I wouldn't have to struggle too hard to find a small degree of legitimacy in his rancor.

MG: I'm surprised. I didn't honestly realize the depths, or the heights, of my hostility until I submitted to this interview.

FB: I'm sorry you use the word *submit*. I didn't force you, Max. I didn't twist your arm.

MG: I apologize, Forest. I obviously wanted to talk about this. But truly, I'm usually free of hostility.

FB: Is it because of him or because of her? Mary Beth Led—

MG: So you know about that, do you?

FB: The rumor mills.

MG: I pray my wife doesn't hear about it. That was quite some time ago.

FB: He replaced you?

MG: Yes. And the bastard ruined her.

FB: Ruined her? How? What do you mean? He didn't convert her to Catholicism or lesbianism.

MG: I'm not sure whether to consider that ironic or moronic. Sorry. Apologies again. You've read his magnificent but venal sonnet called "My Last Duchess?"

FB: I never realized. Of course. Mary Beth. Goddamn. Poor Mary Beth.

MG: She thought he loved her. She thought he might leave his wife and marry her. He'd suggested it, in fact. She would have given up one end of her sexual teeter-totter for Farleigh O'Brien.

FB: Did she tell you that?

MG: She did. I think she's a lesbian not just because she loves women but also because, thanks to Farleigh O'Brien, she now hates men.

FB: She doesn't hate men, but I think that's beside the point. What the hell did Farleigh do to her?

MG: Mine not to reason why, his not to do, and die. I'll save you time and energy, however. Don't ask her.

FB: Max, you loved that woman.

MG: Forest, at that time I think I might have left Coco for Mary Beth Lederberg. I never told Mary Beth or my wife that. I never openly told myself. Why the hell do I tell you? I could say it popped out. Of course, we both know nothing just pops out. No matter. Mary Beth's dying, you know.

FB: I guessed as much. Cancer?

MG: I suggest you ask her.

I've collected my material—notebooks, cassettes, tape recorder—and am on my way down the hall when Max calls me back. He nods, indicating I ought to set up my recorder again, and sit. I do.

MG: I've not been truthful, Forest. Or complete.

FB: Oh? When?

MG: It's not a matter of when. I just didn't explain my anger, or justify it. Justify in my mind, that is.

Farleigh liked to pose as guardian of the rights of the underdog. Part of his sixties Marxist posturing. He was totally unaware of my feelings about Israel and the Arabs. I'd never discussed the matter with him. Had no reason to. I rarely discussed Israel with my own kids. Who am I to say what the Israelis should do? I only know what I read in the newspapers, French and American. And we all know about the reliability of newspapers.

131

In 1973, I went to Israel. Returned to campus just one day before the war began. About three or four days later, early in the morning, I walked into the faculty cafeteria. I ordered breakfast.

I was sitting at the table reading the *New York Times*, waiting for my food. There were several people, faculty, at the various tables. Farleigh called out from across the room, "Hey, Max, what do you think about the Israelis killing civilians?"

I went to his table. He was sitting with two other people. Whom I cannot recall. I was so furious my hands were trembling.

I said, "Suddenly, you're concerned about civilians being killed. So am I, Farleigh. It's outrageous. But where have you been for the last twenty years while Jewish civilians were being killed, you fucking Jew-hater? It comes with mother's milk, doesn't it, Farleigh?"

Forest, in my entire life I've never spoken that way to any human being. I've said the word *fucking* maybe three times in my life. One of the reasons I never translated or taught Genet.

Farleigh came to my table later, tried to apologize. I swore at him again. I never swear, Forest. You know that. I told him to shove his apologies up his ass. I've never mentioned this incident to anyone. Not even to Coco.

FB: Do you honestly think he's...he was...anti-Semitic?

MG: You're going to have me screaming at you. You sure you want to keep that question on the table?

Okay, I'm sure he never thought himself an anti-Semite. But most intellectuals who are not Jews wouldn't recognize anti-Semitism in themselves if they received an electric shock every time a Jew-hating thought came to their mind. Use the story if you wish, though I doubt there's a place for it in a

132

critique of the man's art. But it won't leave my memory. You've been reading the Joseph Campbell flap, haven't you?

According to Brendan Gill of *The New Yorker* the great man hated Blacks and Jews. Does it show in his work? I guess not, but I stopped reading him. Farleigh O'Brien is a far lesser artist. I've stopped caring, or even thinking, about him. I tell you, I'm glad I'm retiring next year.

I decide I've received about as much as is there, and begin gathering my recorder and cassettes and notebook. Max, watching me, holds up his hand just as I am about to close my briefcase.

"Let me say a bit more. A different situation. I discussed this with two colleagues, a few years ago. I've also discussed it with Brother Roderick. You know Brother Roderick and I are friends. He's been denigrated by the faculty but he's a well-intentioned man. Very considerate of others. More considerate, more honorable, than many of my colleagues. Let me give it to you. It's important. To me, at least.

You said you want to know about Farleigh O'Brien. This might help. You can do with it as you wish."

And so I turn on my recorder and put in a new cassette and start recording.

MG: This is less personal than the Israel incident. It's about morality. Farleigh O'Brien was one of the most unprofessional and immoral professors I've ever met.

FB: You mean professional immorality? Did he assault a student? That's moral turpentine, as Paul describes it.

MG: Don't try me, Forest. Do you want to hear this?

FB: I'm sorry. Of course I want to hear it.

MG: Forest, I owe this college, and the Ursuline Brothers, more than I could ever repay. I'm a Jew. They've treated me with decency and sensitivity. You both—you and Paul Scarborough—have contempt for the place.

FB: Max, I didn't realize this was going to be an attack on Paul and me. I don't mind your criticizing me, I'm here, I can defend myself. Paul's not here. He's my oldest and dearest friend, and I won't let you...

MG: My turn to apologize. And I do so. But you have to admit that the two of you have not made the job of the president any easier for Brother Roderick.

FB: Professors are not present at any college to make the job of the president easier. He is there to make the professors' jobs easier. The faculty is the heart of any college. The president is there to get the dollars and pay the bills and keep the heart healthy.

MG: AAUP dogma. You sound like the Stalinists in the thirties and forties. You're just too bright to mouth slogans, Forest.

FB: And you're just too arrogant to think that longevity gives you the right to tyrannize your junior colleagues.

I start to pack up my things again, but I can't take my eyes off Max's wrinkled, wounded face. Max has very few friends left among the faculty. In a year, he'll be gone from here, and just possibly Brother Roderick will be the only person to lament his departure. I sit down again, my recorder turned on.

FB: Let's start over. You've always been helpful when I needed advice, Max. I'm sorry, but Farey's death has unhinged me. I've not been myself. The consequences scare the hell out of me. We were close friends at one time, you know.

MG: Yes, I know. I remember a dinner at your house. The Scarboroughs, you and Emerald, the Spaniels, Mary Beth and Jeanne. You and Scarborough laughed at each other's jokes. My children tell me they have never heard me laugh at a joke. Did you know about Farleigh's role in the Polyfemus promotion?

FB: Wait. About five years ago. Something to do with Polyfemus's tenure.

MG: That's right. I don't know what your feelings are about such things as confidentiality, but I'm a bear on the issue. Details of discussions of any committee, especially the big ones, like Rank and Tenure, must be confidential. The careers of faculty members depend on confidentiality. Professors must be free to make judgments about promotion and tenure without fear that what they say or write about someone will ever be divulged. If confidentiality is broken and leaks occur no one will freely participate in tenure or promotion decisions. They'd be afraid of their words or votes being disclosed. Could cause severe morale problems.

FB: Polyfemus was up for tenure, and O'Brien was on the Rank and Tenure Committee.

MG: Wrong. Polyfemus was up for promotion to full professor. Right, O'Brien was on the committee. He fought for Polyfemus' promotion. But the R and T finally voted to deny promotion.

O'Brien immediately, within minutes after the meeting, went to Brother Roderick. He convinced Brother Roderick that he, the president, ought to override the committee. The president has that power. After all, every committee is only advisory to the president.

Only twice in the last fifteen years has the president over-ridden the R and T Committee. O'Brien is important to this college. He brings prestige and attention. And endowment money.

FB: So, the President gave Polyfemus his promotion to full professor. Max, O'Brien's tactics were tacky, maybe, but not a break of confidentiality. I don't see any major crime here. Not enough to keep me steaming five years after the event.

MG: Tacky? Maybe? A break in confidentiality not a major crime? Why am I wasting my time? You wanted to know why people reacted to O'Brien the way they did. O'Brien's actions illustrate his lack of even the slightest respect for ethical behavior. What would you say if I told you O'Brien and Polyfemus have been close friends since childhood, that they spent their summers together on very expensive ranches up north in the gold country?

What would you say if I told you that Polyfemus was very active, and successful, in getting a Master of Fine Arts program on this campus? What would you say if I tell you that, at the time of the vote, Polyfemus already had at least five million dollars pledged for a new building to house the MFA program? What would you say if I tell you that Polyfemus had already informed O'Brien that the building would have big beautiful offices and O'Brien was to be chair of the program, with the best and most beautiful office on the entire campus? No break in confidentiality?

What would you say if I told you that O'Brien marched up to Polyfemus's office minutes after he got a promise from Brother President and—a professor in the next office heard this—and said, "You owe me a dinner, Polly. A special one. Let's say Chez Pannisse."

And then he told Polyfemus what had happened, who had voted yes, who had voted no. Still no big deal? You don't feel outraged? You don't see all this as deceit and greed?

FB: You're sure of all this? Was it proven? If it was, I never heard about it. If you're so outraged, why

136

didn't you speak up? If I were a judge, I'd consider you an accomplice in the crime.

MG: I *did* speak up. Without naming names. In the faculty assembly. But since neither you nor Scarborough ever grace the faculty meetings with your presence and obviously never read the notes of our meetings, you aren't, weren't, aware of any of this. I'd suggest, if you're doing a critical study of the man, you do a little old-fashioned spadework.

FB: Max, do you realize that you're letting yourself become a mean old eccentric? Is that the way you want to be remembered?

MG: Frankly, Forest, I don't give a damn how I'm remembered. It's *what* I remember that concerns me.

3/23/93

I thought a great deal about interviewing Paul as I'd interviewed Mary Beth and Max, but Paul Scarborough is my closest friend. An interview could taint that friendship. I know Tony's talked to him. A taped session might suggest to Paul that I also consider him a possible suspect.

Tonight, after the Goldstein interview, and editing it, I am exhausted. I'm not even sure how I'll work the interviews into the novel. Am I trying too hard? Gathering data instead of writing? Am I simply searching for distractions? Get your ass on that chair, Forest!

I decide to delay the interview with Paul, to rely on what I already know about him. Over the next few weeks, while I get into the novel, I'll be talking to him a great deal.

3/24/93

I haven't seen Leslie Costello for a year, but I have my notes from our conference. Here they are, and I can guarantee they're as true an account as if it had been taped. One of the benefits of being a professor and a critic is that my notes are even more reliable perhaps than a tape because I detail the nuances of expression, body language, mood that a tape cannot pick up.

3. LESLIE COSTELLO

5/12/92

Leslie was in one of my Faulkner classes when she was a sophomore. She is now a senior, graduating in May. Very bright, driven by intense emotions, yearns to be a poet. Or yearned. Poetry has been an obsession ever since she was in grade school. During her freshman and sophomore years she was one of my advisees but when, in her third year, she began to take classes from O'Brien, she chose to have him for her advisor. She assured me her change was not personal.

"You're great, Professor Butler, but Farleigh's a poet, a really great poet, you know, and he's really helped me a lot. I mean he's just a...he's got a poet's soul. You know? Please understand."

Yes, indeed. I know. Or rather, knew. I understood. Leslie had never been political. She'd certainly never been an activist. But that semester, when she was in O'Brien's class, she was the most fiery and articulate activist during the rape crisis.

That rape crisis provoked a spontaneous protest by a group of students, mostly women, against the sudden outburst of sexual and physical assault on the campus. Leslie was present at every meeting whether it was called by faculty, students or administration. Unintimidated, she met with reporters from newspapers and television.

The administration was furious with her, and with a few of the faculty who also went public, willingly contributing to the media assault, which, of course, could seriously effect new-student enrollment. Her poems, published in the *Cross and Trumpet*, the campus newspaper, were as strident and forceful as the writings of the most angry and hostile feminists in the country. She also printed broadsheets that were stapled to every flat surface on campus.

After the crisis began to resolve Leslie seemed to lose power. She retired, became her old quiet, introverted self. I used to see her every day, at one protest or another, but then I didn't see her at all.

Leslie's mother and father are committed Catholics. They have strong ties to Italy, with several uncles, aunts and cousins still there. Her father called me soon after the crisis, very concerned about Leslie, who had been quite ill for several days. She'd left her campus room and was living at home. She'd always admired me and talked about me. Did I have any idea about her sudden weirdness, as he called it?

I tried to reassure him, reminding him Leslie was a very sensitive young woman, at the height of her idealism, but I knew she was devoted to her family and to the church. I was sure she'd recover fully and rapidly. She returned to campus soon after, a quieter, more restrained Leslie.

But then one of her roommates, a biology major, came to talk to me. Her name was Jefferson. Candace Jefferson. That was near the end of the semester, about two weeks before I began my sabbatical. Leslie's room mate was worried about her. Would I talk to Leslie, even though she was no longer my advisee? Of course I would.

Candace made an appointment. She'd convince Leslie to come see me. Leslie did not show up. I called her. Candace answered. She was surprised to learn Leslie had not kept her appointment. Yes, Leslie seemed much better these days. Much less depressed. She had attributed Leslie's improvement to our meeting. She said she'd make Leslie call me back.

I think Candace actually did walk her to my door that time. I had no reason to consider using a tape recorder, but I couldn't have used one anyway. It would have betrayed Leslie's trust.

So I write this now as an accurate record of the meeting. Accurate because often, with or without the knowledge of people, I recorded our conversations. Occasionally, when someone expressed concern, I reassured them by, one, guaranteeing absolute confidentiality and, two, by promising copies of the transcribed discussion. Rarely did trusting students ask for a copy.

My explanation for using a recorder: should our conversation ever be needed by one or the other to verify statements, by either party, in a disagreement—about grades, about behavior, about exchange of confidences—the tape would offer support to both parties. Perhaps because I've always had a premonition that I'd be writing a novel some day.

FB: Leslie, I'm glad you came.

LC: I'm sorry about that appointment.

FB: That's okay. Your parents were worried about you. So was your roommate.

LC: Candace. My best friend ever. I had a hard time for a couple weeks, but I'm okay now. Call it life experience.

FB: I've never heard cynicism in your voice before.

LC: Imagine. Jaded at the age of twenty-two.

FB: Hey, come on. You behaved very well. And the college agreed to almost everything you and your friends demanded. You can be proud of yourself. I— and most of my colleagues—are impressed with you and all the students. Maybe you're just burned out. It's temporary. Believe me. You'll wake up one morning, totally recovered, ready to go again.

LC: Burned out? *Burned up*'s a better phrase. That is a phrase, isn't it? I keep forgetting the difference between a phrase and a clause.

FB: What's happened, Leslie? You seem so...well, so alone. A lot of people care about you.

LC: Professor Butler...

FB: Most of the students call me Forest. After all these years, why don't you?

LC: I know. Students trust you. I feel like a traitor, leaving you to go—

FB: Leaving me?

LC: To go to Farleigh O'Brien. You'd always been there when I needed help or advice or just support. And then zap, I just run right to him, chase after him. Like everyone else.

Leslie bursts out weeping. I find some tissue for her, but it is several minutes before she can talk. Something of great importance, great at least to Leslie, must have occurred between her and Farleigh. My first thought is he'd seduced her. She idolized him, she was so vulnerable. Had he raped her? Was that the source of her dedication to the rape-and violence issue?

FB: Can you tell me what happened, Leslie? I'm not a therapist, but I listen well. Sometimes, that's even more important. And there's no charge.

LC: Okay. Well, when I registered for his poetry class, it wasn't like it was a Mickey Mouse course. Students say that. It was...well, ever since I was nine years old, maybe ten, I wanted to be a poet. Mother's Day, Father's Day, birthdays—I'd write poems and frame them. Everyone would say they were special gifts. I won prizes in grade school and high school. I even went to bookstores and bought books of poetry. You know Rod McKuen? My mom took me to hear him read his poetry once. Wow. I kept his book next to my bed like it was a bible.

First two years I was here, I kept trying to get into Farleigh's class, but there was always a line ahead of me. And I wasn't an English major. So what happens? In my junior year, I get in.

I was in heaven. Lots of times he wasn't in class. Like he was at some other college giving readings. He even went to Europe. He'd get friends to take over his classes. They were usually okay, but they, you know, weren't Farleigh O'Brien. We'd all registered for that class to be with the famous Farleigh O'Brien.

Once, there was a woman poet from San Francisco, he'd said she was a strong feminist and a very fine poet. I was impressed. She wasn't Farleigh O'Brien, but she said things I'd never heard before. Or thought about.

FB: Do you remember her name?

LC: Sure. Mimi Fa la la.

FB: A Black woman?

LC: Yeah. Very tough. Made you think.

But sometimes when he didn't show up no one covered for him, and the department secretary would come in and say we were to do projects in the library. You know—read someone or listen to poets on records. That sort of thing.

But some students complained. A couple went to the chairman. Wanted their money back. The chairman couldn't care less. They went to administration. They couldn't care less. The famous Farleigh O'Brien brought all sorts of fame to the college. He could do anything.

And it was the students' fault, too. He was so great when he was there, he'd just win us over. We forgave him. He was a poet. You can't expect poets to be responsible. He used to joke about that, but we all knew he believed it.

Anyway, when he was there, he was so kind and so helpful, and he was like one of those old-timey preachers you hear about. You know, in tents. People treated them like they were gods or something. That's the way Farleigh was. You'd come out of his class some days just sure that poetry could save the word.

Most English classes are, you know, ordinary. You read a lot, you talk a lot, you write a paper, you get a grade. No big deal. But Farleigh's class was different. It really was sort of like going to church. You know? You felt clean and full of energy and love afterward. You wished people in politics were there listening to Farleigh O'Brien, talking to him. There'd never be wars or race riots.

FB: Did you write a lot of poetry? Did he talk to you about your writing?

LC: Hey, I wrote poetry day and night. I'm a business major, and I cut econ and accounting classes, and I wrote poetry. All the time.

And it wasn't just happy birthday stuff anymore. Farleigh talked in class about the Feminist Movement, and we read a lot of women poets. Feminists. He was always talking about women on campus getting sensitized. He talked about the school not helping women. The rapes, the first rape—there were others later—Farleigh told us, told me, that's what we ought to be writing about. Get sensitized!

I loved that word. Sensitized. I sat up all night. I didn't do anything else. I wrote poetry. I wanted Farleigh to praise me. He did, too. I saw him alone in his office three times, and he just raved about my poetry.

How'd he say it? My "getting a grip on my feelings that I'd kept hidden down in my guts all my life."

Man, I ate it up. I ate, slept, talked Farleigh O'Brien. I was his star. I dreamed about him. I had real, you know, erotic dreams about him. He was always saying, "Get your feelings out there."

So, I told him about my dreams. He didn't laugh or pat me on the head, he didn't embarrass me. I knew it was a sin, but I wanted him to take me to bed so badly. I shivered just sitting beside him.

Later, afterwards, I realized he was getting off on that. I know it, I really do. One day, in class, one of the guys wrote a poem about his girlfriend, how they both got drunk, and he left her out in the woods when she wouldn't put out.

That's how he said it. When she wouldn't put out. She had to walk home through the woods about three miles. Lots of the guys in class laughed. Farleigh really went after the poet and his buddies. The women, especially me, we were saying, yeah yeah yeah, go get the bastards, Farleigh.

FB: What eventually happened?

LC: I believed everything he said. About my poetry, I mean.

FB: He probably meant it.

LC: No, he didn't. When Candi—next to Debby, my really best friend—she was beaten up by her boyfriend and almost raped. She ran from the car and called me, and I picked her up and drove her back to campus.

I ran to Farleigh the next day for help, I even wrote a real angry poem about it. Farleigh loved my poem, wanted me to read it to the class. I couldn't. He was so mad about what happened to Candi he promised to go right to the president's office.

Well, Candi's dad's a lawyer. He flew up from LA. That's when it hit the fan. In two days, other women were talking about how they'd been beaten up or raped or both. It snowballed. Big meetings at night in the dorms.

FB: That's when the faculty got involved.

LC: After seven women got raped. I remember the faculty's petition. It went to the editor of the paper. There were about twenty-five signatures. Out of what? A hundred-fifty? The paper printed it. I saw your name on it.

FB: The entire English department signed it.

LC: Even Old Sourpuss, Professor Scarborough. And Farleigh signed it. And Professor Goldstein.

But then there were more women telling more stories. And there was that protest. Just about all the women on campus. Some men, too, but mostly women. We marched to the president's office. Then the media got hold of it. TV, radio, newspapers, they all came on campus. First local, then national. All the big networks.

Another friend, Sandy Corino, told her parents about a football player beating her up and raping her. Her aunt's real rich. She's on the board of trustees of the college. She was furious. She called a special meeting of the trustees. The administration squirmed and squealed and tried to blame us, the women. We wore improper clothes, we drank, we had guys in our rooms. A priest—at a mass, mind you, at a mass—denounced the faculty. You weren't Christians. That's what he said. We weren't Christians.

After that, all of a sudden, Farleigh was careful. You know, detached. He wouldn't be interviewed by any of the media people. He was the biggest name on campus, that's why they went after him. But no interviews. He wouldn't even answer his phone. He wouldn't see me after classes. When we talked, at his desk, his hands shook. In class, he'd not even call on me.

Hey, he'd been bragging and writing about being a feminist—in class he was always talking like he was furious about how men treat women—but now he had to put his money where his mouth was. I think he was afraid his name would be tarnished. Maybe he was afraid he'd lose this great job, you know, where he can do anything he wants. Not even come to class if he wants.

He stopped talking to me about everything, even my poetry, until I confronted him one day in his office. I was writing about the rapes on campus. Articles in the newspaper, petitions, poems in class. That sort of stuff. I was...I guess you could say I was strident. But I asked him directly. Did he still like my poetry? He told me to grow up, stop screaming, and you know what? He looked like he was going to hit me once.

"Tell those goddamn reporters to leave me alone. You sent them after me, you call them off." Then he sort of got hold of himself. He looked friendly, even sort of held my hand. You know what he said? He said, "You'd be better off to forget this so-called issue."

FB: So-called issue?

LC: His words. Can you believe it? He said there wasn't proof that would hold up in a courtroom that any student had been raped. It was all—what do you call it?

FB: Hearsay?

LC: Hearsay, right. That's when I really lost it. I told him off. Said he was a damn phony. I called him every name I could think of. I couldn't care less. I said—it wasn't true, but I said it—I said the students were getting ready to go on strike, and every member of his class was going to expose him.

FB: Expose him? For what?

LC: Nothing. It wasn't going to happen. It just came out of my mouth. We didn't have anything to expose. I was just, you know, striking out.

But you should have seen his face. He looked like all of a sudden we knew some big dark secret about him. His hands were shaking, he stammered, his eyes got all teary.

He said, "Leslie, try to calm down. You're making yourself sick. I'll tell you what. I'll talk to my colleagues and the administration. Be patient."

What did he do? That afternoon he called a meeting of the instructors and administration people to talk about the rape crisis. *He* called the meeting. Who was he to call a meeting? I couldn't believe the guy. Did he talk to any students? Any women students? No. He didn't even invite any students to his meeting. And it really was *his* meeting.

FB: I remember. But there were students there. Hundreds of them.

LC: Right. *I* invited them. And he chewed me out. I mean, he said I was a troublemaker, I had no right inviting students, this was a meeting for faculty. I screamed at him, "Name me one instructor including you who's been raped."

He was always preaching about victims having a voice in the laws that govern them. I told him that. He just walked away from me.

When he finally did take over the meeting, he tried to speak for the women. Can you believe it? Nobody had elected him to take over, to represent the women, he said what he thought they'd want to say. Him, of all people, speaking for women.

Then he handled the meeting the way the seminar's conducted. You know: "You talk, now you, now you." He was the self-appointed little dictator. I was sick, honest-to-God sick. I had to leave.

That's when I went home and stayed home. I feel so dumb. If my parents would let me I'd quit school tomorrow.

Leslie begins weeping again. What the hell had O'Brien done to her?

FB: Leslie, talk to me about it.

She keeps weeping, partly, I think, because she is still suffering from whatever had occurred and partly from her now separate humiliation. She's exposed her own failings to herself, and what is worse, I'd guess, she is exposing her weakness to me. But what the hell could that "weakness" be?

FB: Have you talked to your parents? Your roommate? You can talk to me. I won't judge you. Hell, I'm not just a professor, Leslie, I'm a loco in parentis. In Latin that means I'm sort of a substitute parent. It means you can trust me even more than you can your own parents because I'm sort of loco.

She tries to laugh, tries to stop weeping, accepts another tissue, and then nods.

LC: I guess he was scared. Maybe the college had gotten to him. You know, the administration. Maybe...I don't know what. I just know I was so...so...so devastated I almost went crazy.

After that big meeting he went off somewhere to give a reading. Iowa, I think. When he came back he missed two classes. I ran into him in the hall one day. His hands were shaking. In class he'd never call on me. He'd stopped talking to me about anything.

So, that day I just waited after class. We were alone. I'd written this really important story for the newspaper that came out that day. I'd quoted him, things he'd said in class, about becoming sensitized, about women empowering themselves. I always wrote down everything he said in class so I had it word for word. I really begged him to talk to me.

He got his face up almost right against mine. "Leslie, if you don't back off, if you don't get off my ass, I'll flunk you. You hear me, Leslie? I'll flunk your ass."

He looked like...like maybe he was ready to hit me. I was scared. I thought, Farleigh O'Brien's crazy, he's really crazy.

But then, you know, I didn't care. I went from fear right to anger. I was so damn mad I wanted to kill him. I really did. I could have just, you know, stood there watching him suffer while I killed him.

I said, "Some day I'm going to get you. I'm going to destroy you."

Well, like, I was crazy then. I never went near him again. Never went to class, never talked to him, never handed in any work. I missed the last three weeks of class. He gave me a B+. I think it was a goddamn bribe. Sorry.

Leslie is weeping. I hand her more tissues. She stops, waits, recovers, in control again. She gives a deep sigh and stands up.

"Phew. I feel better. I better go, before I make a bigger idiot of myself. Thanks, Professor...Forest. I changed back to you for my advisor. Hope you don't mind."

She giggles, as if she'd just played a prank on her boyfriend and is now going out to get a Coke. She rushes back, hugs me, says I'm a doll, and this time she does leave.

Looking over this exchange now, I think most of it's there. Leslie is young, very emotional, unpredictable, very malleable. Could she be a potential killer? Not

149

the real Leslie but a Leslie (call her something like Patti or Cindy or Debbi) I could create? She said she wanted to. Hells bells, the hormones that make an adolescent or college kid throw him(her)self in front of a troop train to stop the war could just as easily buy, beg, borrow, steal a handgun and shoot a professor.

Okay, I have my killer. A vulnerable, impassioned, idealistic young student. Readers will sympathize with her. Anyone mistreating such a little gem of a girl deserves to be shot. Right? Right!

CHAPTER 8

3/25/93

As with the others: a forward. An introduction. I decide to go ahead and interview Paul Scarborough, expecting nothing new, at least no more than insignificant variations on themes shared over the last thirty years. I called Paul and told him what I was doing and why. He was prepared, of course.

"I volunteer to be your next victim," he said. "It's necessary, Forest."

He agreed that we should treat the interview without bias, as if I were as socially and psychologically removed from him as I was from Mary Beth and Max and Leslie.

Paul Scarborough and I arrived at Saint Catherine's the same year—1968. The English department was struggling for recognition as a serious collegiate haven for graduates (male) from Catholic high schools, and the two of us brought credentials that promised academic sanctification. Paul had his degree from Princeton and was an author of two books and many articles on what the journals and our colleagues referred to as Victorian literature.

"Not Victorian," he insisted the day we met, "the nineteenth century."

For Paul the nineteenth century was never proper, as the word *Victorian* has come to suggest. The Victorian patina of propriety covered a society that was raunchy and rambunctious and unconventionally radical.

As a graduate student, I'd read a great deal of Dickens, had even considered an article arguing that Twain's stories and characters had a perverse familial relationship to the British master, with both relying on caricature to attract attention so they could more safely sneer at the worst elements of their societies. When Paul confessed that the idea had merit I deferred to him. He ended up producing a much admired (and far more elegant) argument than I could ever have managed.

Maria had been one of Paul's graduate students who, four months into their affair, became pregnant. She used the fact not so much as a hasty excuse to get married as to quit school, for which she'd had little patience and less interest. Her education had been earned before she came to college, when she'd lived with one of the leaders of the rebellion at Berkeley.

"Imagine," Paul crowed, "I'm a father at the same age my father was a grandfather. Too bad he's not alive to advertise my virility. Well, I am. Have a second cigar."

Maria has acclimated to Paul's often nasty wit and occasionally annoying eccentricities at home and abroad, but whenever she feels so inclined, she can destroy him with the iciest glare a human eye has ever devised. One of their children, a daughter, is a graduate student at Wellesley and the other, a son, is a landscape architect.

"Which means he cuts grass," Paul said.

"Poor man," Maria added, "he can't get fixed to anything that moves without driving it into the ditch. He's on his third pickup this year."

Unlike me, Paul had been in the service. The Korean war. He'd been in the Marines, in fact, and had actually participated in what must have been serious combat on the Inchon Peninsula. He was a lieutenant, I know, but much of the little I know I learned from my interview with Max Goldstein. Paul's not talked about it very much, but it's obvious he's embittered by the experience, feeling that, like the Vietnam war, the Korean war had been suspect and the returning veterans never did receive the honor received by those who had served in the so-called Second World War.

He has no patience with what he terms "the whining Vietnam vets."

"Their suffering was no more calamitous than the suffering of any man who's seen action on the front lines in any war. So, we lost the war in Vietnam. We didn't lose it. *They* did—those Macnamaras and Bundys and Kissingers who wasted fifty thousand men for their own egos and pocketbooks and are now very rich, very comfortable, very safe elder statesmen. They never had to face their Nuremberg. Blame your enemies, crybabies, not your friends."

Paul and I have been colleagues, allies, friends, for almost thirty years, but I honestly admit that I rely on him for understanding and support much more than he relies on me. I think he could, in fair contentment, remain at Saint Cate's without my being there. I cannot imagine my having endured thirty years without Paul available for my prayers and confessions. He supported me in my two ill-fated attempts to write those novels and stroked my wounded psyche when, finally, I had to admit failure.

At the age of almost forty, with Paul and Maria already anticipating their children leaving home, I married Emerald. Paul honored my request for secrecy. I don't know if he's ever told Maria that I met Emerald through an ad for "Available Asian Ladies." Maria, always discrete, has never mentioned it to me nor, so far as I know, to Emerald. She could have taken for granted that we'd met at some academic function.

With the two women exchanging an immediate affection for each other, they have gone on, over the years, to spend much time together, occasionally taking long weekend trips to Los Angeles or Seattle. I've never asked Maria if Emerald has enlightened her. More than once, however, usually after the one-over-the-limit drink, Maria has often congratulated me on my good fortune.

"You're just lucky I'm not gay," she confided once, about three years after I married Emerald.

❦

I interview Paul at home.

The Scarboroughs live in the Berkeley Hills, as we do, though their house is much larger and more contemporary. Ours, a Victorian spawned by a hallucinatory marriage of Julia Morgan and Bernard Maybeck, is a very large collection of sunlit redwood rooms tied together by long shadowed hallways and two spiraling staircases and (this was Maybeck's influence, not Morgan's) a kitchen the size of a shoebox.

Paul smokes his pipe throughout the interview. Again: only the essentials as they bear on M by M.

FB: When Tony called you, were you surprised?

Paul Scarborough: Nothing relating to Farleigh O'Brien surprises me. You know that. I think Tony was surprised when I'd not tell him what I was doing in San Francisco that morning. He was very careful to assure me I was not a suspect, but I might have to come in for some routine questioning. I said only if I was subpoenaed. All in all, he was more respectful than a cop has the right to be. He should have threatened to break my face or beat me with a kippered herring or turn me into a boy soprano. I want him to play the role if we're going to do this right.

FB: Don't you find it difficult to believe that someone might have murdered O'Brien? I think only traitorous spies and stupid drug dealers are murdered in their homes.

PS: I would not be surprised if Farleigh turns out to have been both.

FB: Okay, you read my interview with Leslie. Could I make Leslie a credible killer?

PS: I can't imagine any student from Saint Catherine's College getting out of bed early enough to drive across the bridge to get there at the time the coroner says O'Brien died. She would have had to have stayed with the bastard all night. Feeling the way she says she did, I doubt she would have gotten close enough to him to smell his breath.

FB: She never slept with him. She said so, and I believe her. I'd bet she's one of three virgins on campus.

PS: So? Are you writing a biographical novel? Remember Creative Writing 101 your freshman year? You don't have to have your novel's Leslie do what the real Leslie did. But don't listen to me, I'm a professor. I'm not an expert on writing novels. Like all the other assholes in every college English department in the country, I'm only an expert on how they should be written.

FB: The real Leslie's a good model. My novel's Leslie will have the real Leslie's youth and ideals and devastating, self-destructive emotions. No suspect—at least none of Tony's suspects, none of you three—are as filled with hate and anger as Leslie is.

155

PS: Hey, don't sell my hate and anger short or cheap.

FB: Why would Paul Scarborough want to kill Farleigh O'Brien?

PS: Because Paul Scarborough hated the bastard. Because Paul Scarborough had long-standing scores to settle with Farleigh O'Brien.

FB: What scores? You and I indulged Farleigh O'Brien for almost fifteen years. Why, suddenly, would you be moved to shoot him in the head?

PS: I'll tell you.

Paul puts down his pipe and opens a drawer in his desk. He pulls out a packet of photographs of a handsome man. He throws them in a sort of gambler's toss, letting the cards fall as they may.

There are seven photographs, all of them black-and-white except for the last one, a Polaroid. The young boy in one grade-school photograph becomes a high school graduate in cap and gown, then a business executive, then a retired golfer, then a sick old sad-eyed man in a wheelchair about to die.

PS: In his last years, my brother Harvey, whom I loved very much, wrote poetry. Bad poetry. But poetry important to him. He was trying to understand why he'd become a useless bored and boring old eccentric and I'd become "a happy man." His term. He didn't know.

FB: You sent him some of Farleigh's poetry.

PS: I sent him everything O'Brien had ever published at that time. That was soon after O'Brien came to Saint Cate's.

Harvey read every poem, every line, every word. He wanted to know all about Farleigh. How he lived, how he got his ideas for poems, how he wrote, what he looked like. I answered all his letters as well as I could.

After I told Farleigh about him, I spent a lunch period one day interviewing Farleigh, getting the information Harvey wanted. Farleigh was as sympathetic as a father, a brother. He suggested he write Harvey. I was very pleased and gave him the address.

I told Harvey he'd be hearing from O'Brien. Harvey was ecstatic. He sat patiently in his wheelchair every day. The arrival of the mailman was the nucleus of each day's life.

FB: I can guess what happened.

PS: I bet you can. O'Brien didn't write. I gently reminded him. He promised to write that night. He didn't.

Paul collects the photographs, handling them as if they might crumble if they're treated too roughly. He settles them in the drawer and slams the drawer shut.

PS: A measly fucking letter he could have dashed off in ten minutes. But there wasn't anything in it for Farleigh. Harvey Scarborough couldn't get him published or get him a grant or a medal. The son of a bitch. My brother Harvey died waiting for the mailman.

Tough, cynical, bitter, even mean Paul Scarborough turns away. If I didn't know him I could swear his eyes are filled with tears.

I have a sudden terrifying belief that Paul *had* killed O'Brien. I thank him, offer to buy him lunch the next day. Off campus. He shakes his head, congratulates me for not wanting to be on campus until I have to be. We'll see each other on Thursday, at our place. Emmy and Maria are sharing the dinner preparations.

I come home feeling a bit sick. I take a nap, wake up about mid-afternoon and get to work on the novel. I don't want to interview anyone else. I want to write all day, all night. I want to finish the novel in a single marathon run at the computer.

CHAPTER 9

Forest, by the day, hour, minute, loses interest in his article on Twain. Twain, publication, academic credentials, the college are no more significant in his life these days than Stendahl's gonorrhea. Or was it syphilis?

Like a mass of iron filings swarming with unprincipled resistance toward a concealed magnet, his thoughts, his dreams, his journal entries, his conversations (especially with Paul) cluster about his yet-to-be written novel.

Novel!

Novel novel novel. If his theory of Twain's fraud is correct, and if he is the only scholar in the world collecting data to prove it, the date of the article's publication will be insignificant, as, in the long run of academic events, the article itself can be. Should he feel the need to return to it later, after his novel is published, his fame can only bring more attention to his explosive discoveries about the Zeus of American literature.

Had he been in the slightest doubt about the need for his novel, the interviews with Mary Beth

Lederberg and Max Goldstein have given final reassurance. The interviews have accomplished something else, something unexpected—they have actually given flesh to what might be called (what Forest might call) the skeleton of his story.

As a student of creative writing when he was a freshman, a famous novelist had visited his class. "Remember," the famous novelist had advised the budding writers, "an idea for a story is a dry skeleton. A skeleton is just bones. You add tissue, muscle, brain. That means people, characters who do things to other people. Readers, being people, can identify with your characters, whom you've just made people. What you make your characters say and think and feel and do makes them attractive or ugly. Be passionate about the people you create because you are now God."

Almost thirty-five years ago, yet Forest, recalling every detail of the famous writer's advice, finds it just as meaningless now as he found it then.

That famous novelist was a *New York Times* Best Seller institution, and he was full of shit.

Had he, Forest wondered, ever been passionate about the important matters of his life? His experiments with his own body had begun relatively late in his adolescence, had been infrequent and almost incidental, carried out not because the intense sensations proved exciting but because he knew he was obligated to perform them while en route to the distant station called manhood. Often, during the sixties, while he was picking his way through the minefields of graduate school at Berkeley, friends and colleagues would scurry off to peace marches or draft protests or rock concerts. Forest stayed home and read *Goncharov* by Oblamov. Or was it *Oblamov* by Goncharov?

There were times when he almost envied his activist friends. At least they were out in the fresh air. He tried to participate two or three times, but he might just as well have played pool or gone to a bad movie.

He did sign several petitions supporting free speech, and once, after a threat of bodily harm from Sarah Ormsby, a pretty student he was occasionally sleeping with, he had actually (or was her name Sally?) joined Sarah's (or Sally's) brigade of picketers who blocked the campus entrance at the university's Sather Gate. And wow! Did he feel virtuous!

But should the Oakland police and marshals—sun-glassed giants in blue jumpsuits called the Blue Meanies—gather him up in their promised sweep and haul him away to Santa Rita Prison, they would find his pants not just wet but soiled.

They did make their sweep, but their sweep missed both him and Sarah, or Sally; and that night in bed, on the ground behind the Life Sciences Building, under a lilac tree ("*Ceonothus Californicus,*" Sarah intoned as she rose to meet his descent), he discovered why young boys masturbated and adults fornicated. A cyclone born in his toes swept up through his crotch and gathered his head in a swirl that tore his head from his neck.

"You sounded like someone was frying your brain in boiling oil," Sarah (Sally—or was it Stephanie?) whispered into his ear. "Jesus, how long has that been in there?"

The day after one of his protest marches, when he was on the streets again, after having evaded the Blue Meanies a second time, he returned to his room filled with zeal for the anti-war cause. Sarah Sally Stephanie came over to prepare a spaghetti supper. After the food was eaten and the wine drunk, Sarah

Sally Stephanie reminded him, they would run the streets again.

"We have to put our asses on the line." That was the way Sarah (Yes, it had been Sarah—she'd been a wild-eyed Afroed blonde from Fairfield) had put it.

After supper, permitting themselves one final celebratory fuck before storming the barricades, Forest could not manage to, as Sarah said, "Get it up." She pulled on her tattered jeans.

"No sweat. Too much garlic in the spaghetti sauce. Let's go hit the streets, man."

Passion.

He discovered passion again late in life. Not discovered but learned. From Emerald Hyashi.

Three days after he met the delicate Japanese beauty at the San Francisco airport they were in bed in the Claremont Hotel. He was, at her insistence, working on her pronunciation of pecker. And of balls. Of clitoris. "Forest, I want you be purowdu my Engarishu."

"Say *critic*, Emerald. No, no. Kir. Say kir. Now say kir-it-ic. Faster. Kir-it-ic. Critic. Critic. Now say kl. Class. Say kill. Kill-ass. Kill-ass. Fine. Now say kill-it. Kill-it. Excellent. Now kill-it-or-iss. Again. Now: clit-or-is."

Finally, at the exploded *caritorisu*, they both laughed. Thirty-eight years old, he persisted through the night with teenage potency, reducing the ecstatic Emerald to exhausted pleas for mercy.

"Too much for me," she gasped in the early morning. "Too much. You are like a boo."

"A boo?"

"A boo. Cow with baws."

Moved to excessive delight at this ninety-pound kewpie doll, Forest had to have her one more time, after which he bounced on the bed like a nine-year-old, Emerald's eyes rising and falling as he leaped up and came down, grunting, his cock flapping like a piece of loose string. Until the desk called to inform him the people in the neighboring rooms and the room below were complaining. He stood before the mirror and boxed with his image while Emerald slept.

"I'm going to marry you," he told the reflection of the sleeping brown sea-nymph in the bed behind his back.

Now Forest, enjoying the reminiscence, wonders what that visiting famous writer would make of all that. Any of that usable in *Murder by Metaphor*, Mister Famous Writer?

No.

Ah, but those interviews. There's the treasure!

An interesting reaction now as Forest considers those interviews. He perceives, feels, sense, imagines, wonders about, a hint of a possible structure that might be called plot—a series of related actions that begin and end with the student killing the famous poet. But he is a bit leery of the word *plot* right now. In fact, he does not even want to think about it right now.

The plot will shape itself in its own good time. When its shape is final, it will announce itself—*Here I am, Forest! I am The Plot!*—he will recognize it and welcome it like a long-lost love returned.

Then, a traveler relying on a precisely drawn map, he will move from Action A to Action B and on through the alphabet.

In those previous two novels (please try to forget them, Forest!) he had found his way as he wrote, convinced that fiction relies not on research and argument and proof but only on intuition. Oh, and a sense of the difference between a subject and a verb, a phrase and a clause, a sentence and a paragraph. Fiction is such a long-lost cousin (a troubled and discomfiting relative) of academic writing that he had conscientiously *not* given time and thought to anything but the piling up of sentences and the accumulating of pages.

Those first two novels? An editor at Harper who had read both of them said, "They suffer from the same disease (inherited from the same parent, perhaps?) called crap."

An editor at Knopf who read both of them said, "Did an English professor write these novels? What college? I want to know so my child doesn't ever go there."

An editor at Random House said, "No bone and no muscle, not even any skin."

Simon and Schuster's editor (about his second novel): "I'm so infected by your confident knowledge of what is to happen next that I myself have no curiosity about what your characters expect or hope. I never ask, 'And now what happens...now what happens?' See E.M. Forster's *Aspects of the Novel.* Sorry. This writer's story goes dull around page four."

A few students in Leonard Hawksley's English 106 ("Writing Fiction") were Forest's advisees. He knew they learned early in the semester that the writer must rely on the forces of imagination and intuition, which take turns sharing first and second levels of importance. Hawksley's banner, which every student was advised to crochet and hang on the wall: "Outlines stifle spontaneity." Forest has been tempted to show his manuscript to Hawksley eventually but advice, and even possibly criticism, from a man not much more than half his age would be too painful.

Paul Scarborough, about the second novel only because he had never been informed about the first attempt until after Forest had burned it: "Let me see it when it's ready, for Chrissake. You always show me your articles and your books before your final draft. This is a novel. It's writing and it's in my native tongue, isn't it? Imaginative? Creative? Don't use those crutches, Forest. You're a force in American literary criticism. Your ego ought to be impervious by now."

"My ego is like a maidenhead. It's never impervious."

"I think," Paul says, "I'll find a way to use that in one of my classes. I'll quote you. 'As Professor Forest Butler, my colleague and a famous novelist, says...'"

~≋~

The evening of the day he interviewed Max Goldstein, Forest arrives home to find Emerald in the bathtub, somewhere inside a cloud of foam and steam.

"Emerald, you're home early. What happened? I had a fascinating interview with Max Goldstein. He hates Farleigh O'Brien. But now I wonder about Mary Beth's story about—"

"I quit."

Forest sits on the toilet seat, waiting to be assured that he has misunderstood, says, "I thought you said you quit."

"I quit. I say 'quit.' Not fired. Quit. Gave two week...the word? Notice? Two week notice."

Emerald appears truly serene. Not apprehensive, as has so often been the case when, ever since the day she was hired, she has talked about the probability of her being fired because of "my Engarish skiws."

Her income has not ever been essential for their livelihood, but the job itself, her working on her own, has been essential for Emerald's continuing pride in her becoming American. America: where success on the job is a verification of intelligence and skill.

And Emerald Hyashi Butler has, indeed, been successful. She has, almost single-handedly, elevated

165

the investment company of Breitbach, Lomax and Cudahy to, if not one of the Fortune 500, at least one of the *San Francisco Chronicle* 10. Assured by both Breitbach and Lomax and, finally, by Cudahy, that she has a job for life, Emerald has continued to struggle to prove her competence.

But Emerald, influenced by the suspicions of her friend Maria Scarborough—"They—Breitbach and Lomax, especially—are only flattering you when they praise you. Why else would Cudahy comment, so often, on your beauty? Me, I am always wary of geeks bearing gifts."

"Geeks? Breit Lomax, Cudahy not from Greece, Maria."

Forest—oh, yes, and Paul, when given the opportunity—have always known that Emerald Butler Hyashi would be beyond value for any employer not alone for her beauty.

But Emerald has, she has just informed Forest, quit.

"What did they say when you told them?"

Emerald lowers herself into the foam again until she is out of sight. One...two...three...Her feet kick the water and her head appears, an impish grin on the full pink lips. With her glossy black hair, her flushed cheeks, her small delicate body, she looks like a ten-year-old schoolgirl about to plead for one more doll.

"They offered higher sarry. My own secretary. I say, 'No, thanks.'"

"Well, do you finally believe you're good? Are you convinced now? I've been telling you for years..."

"I say, 'No, thank you very much, I want to write a book.'"

Fortunately, Forest stops his laughter before it erupts, and also fortunately, Emerald sinks into the foam again, missing the sight of his dropped jaw, his attempts to suck in all the air available in the room

166

as well as the rest of the house. She, Emerald Hyashi, who still carries an English dictionary, the Random House Manual and *Strunk and White* when she visits her parents in Japan, who consults both dictionary and manual before writing her letters to Forest and other friends—she, Emerald Hyashi, presumes, pre-fucking-sumes, that she can, will, must, write a novel. Jesus H. Christ! All gall is not divided.

Forest had given Emerald a paperback copy of *Strunk and White's Elements of Style* but because it was such a small volume, he had included, in the same package, the *Random House Manual of Style*. On the plane, on the Japanese trains, in taxis, Emerald carried both the guide and the manual with the grim righteousness of a pilgrim toting holy books. During the first ten years of their marriage, reading some pages Forest had written at his desk (pages not yet edited) Emerald would call out, "Oh-oh...reference pronoun probrem...dangring participer, dangring participer probrem, Forest...dependent crause probrem..."

Now, she has decided to write a...

"You? You are going to write a novel?"

When her head appears out of the foam, he places the towel in her hands. She wipes her eyes, cavorts in the water like a seal pup, giggles and, in her excitement, promptly reverts to the almost infantile English of her adolescence.

"I worita novera. Nota booka. Novera. Novera diherento sanu booka."

"A novel about?"

"My rihe. Bery imaporatanato I worita booka. I meana novera."

"Your life. Your life? Emerald, a novel must be dramatic. You are a beautiful woman and extremely bright and very passionate about many, many issues, but your life has not been especially dramatic."

"I decide, Foreshota. I stay homu. Every day I worita. You do no hewp me. I write it arone. What is word for by mysew?"

"Arone. You just said it."

"No, no. Other word. Card game. You put seven cards on table, in row."

"Solitaire."

"Soritary. I write it in soritary."

"You mean in solitude."

"That what I say. I write in sorituda. So we bos write noveras in sorituda. Husaband-wife team."

"No, we're not a team. We'll be writing different novels. Neither one of us will be showing the other one his-slash-her work."

"Hish-slas-her. Ha-ha." She slaps the foam with her hands. A bouncy little water-sprite. "Okay. Okay. No fair peeking. You don't rook my writing, I don't rook your writing. Okay?"

"Okay, Emerald."

"Agareement. Now I shop for speciar cerebarationa dinner."

CHAPTER 10

When she returns from her shopping spree, after offering Forest a gift of three hours of uninterrupted work, Emerald comes up the stairs calling,

"We have guest, we have guest, Forest." Resettled, almost perfect graduate-school enunciation.

Emerald, leaning on his desk, re-travels her journey street by street in order to inform him how she happened to find their guest.

"I go down San Pablo Avenue to the Pacific Seafood Company to buy fresh tuna. To the Monterey Market for greens and fruit. Fresh levain at Acme Bakery. I stopped for cafe latte at Cafe Fanny's. I stand at counter I wonder why Americans drink coffee and Japanese drink tea and Germans drink beer and French and Italians drink wine. I hear, 'Hello, Emerald.' I turn. It is a man."

"She didn't recognize me," Tony says, popping into the study.

"Well, it has been two years," Emerald reminds him as she hugs him. Then, to Forest: "Would you recognize him? Look. He's no college student now. You see his car? White—what kind, Tony?"

"Thunderbird," Tony says, winking at Forest.

Forest recognizes him alright, and wonders if it is just chance that brought Tony home for Emerald's celebration of her liberation. Or is he on a police-business mission?

"If I hadn't eaten here before, and didn't know what a great cook Emerald is, I'd probably have said I was on duty or was working on a big case."

"Are you working on big case?" Emerald asks.

"Could be," Tony says.

After she lays out slices of tuna for Tony's sashimi, Emerald, leaving student and professor together, goes into the kitchen to prepare the batter and the oil for the tempura. She is trying to remember a Bruce Springsteen tune by repeating the same line of lyrics over and over.

Tony leans close so only Forest will hear him.

"Does Emerald know we've talked?"

Forest, with a slight movement of his head, indicates she does not. Tony lowers himself into a chair, nodding his satisfaction.

Anthony Coniglio had been a much better than average student at Saint Cate's. He'd been a history major, and then business and, finally, thanks to Forest Butler, an English major. He came into the department with a B average. As Tony's advisor, Forest recognized the unacknowledged but always appreciated gifted student. On the basis of previously graded papers Tony brought with him for judgment, Forest judged that B could only have been a gift.

"Your writing needs work, Anthony. Everywhere. Grammar. Syntax. Spelling. Sentence structure. Organization. And that's for starters."

A grin of approximately two hundred strong white teeth cracked open Anthony's dark face.

"Hey, man, that's why I joined the English department. You gotta recognize your weaknesses to turn them into strengths. Here I am. I'm all yours."

Normally, Forest would have tried to convince such a student to find a more compatible advisor, but there was an innocence about the guy that melted his contempt before it began to form. Coniglio was not performing. He was serious about his perception of the English department being there to teach English, not geology or history.

"I wanted to get in that poet's class. What's his name? Kelly? Shaughnessy?"

"O'Brien?"

"O'Brien. Yeah. But you gotta have a two-year reservation."

"So, I was your second choice."

"Actually third. I went to Professor Scarborough, and after we talked for maybe five minutes he tells me he's already got sixty advisees. He said I ought to talk to you."

"And I thought he was my friend."

"He did say you were the most humane guy on campus."

"Did he tell you to tell me he told you that?"

"Yep."

Anthony Coniglio had not the slightest knowledge of how to be deceitful. He will never grow up to be an academic.

The instructors who'd received and graded Tony's papers had obviously turned away from the effort to judge the writing. They'd given up on the page-after-page of heavy scrawl. The prose—question mark here—consisted of long lines of words (perhaps) linked only by their sharing the same sheet of paper.

But something in Tony's text caught Forest's eye. The innocence and honesty of the young man carried itself onto the paper. He said what he thought with neither restraint nor concern. What you saw was what you got.

And you got what Conrad—or was it Maugham?—once called *heart*. Anthony Coniglio even, when Forest took the time to search out the spaces between words and the stormy splashes of commas and periods, demonstrated a rare (among students) dry wit. An important and distinct point: the texts supposed to be the topics of the papers had obviously been read (half of the battle;) and the writer had tried to think about them (the other half). Proof of his efforts appeared in several rewritten pieces of words and sentences. Re-written and re-rewritten. There were as many pools of cross-hatching as there were shoals of capital letters.

Tony did not make it onto the Dean's list at any time during his four years at Saint Catherine's, but each semester he grew more serious about his studies. He'd begun with what could be called the normal span (for Saint Cate's students) of incompetence—fifth grade-level abilities in spelling and grammar, fourth grade-level in reading, and, along with a second-grade ability to articulate his thoughts, a thorough alienation from what, at most colleges, is normally considered thinking. But his presence asserted itself with a flair that Forest actually envied.

Forest's indulgence expanded into such an interest that he spent more time on private tutoring of Anthony Coniglio than he spent with all other students combined. In less than a month, they were calling each other Forest and Tony.

In his last semester, Tony signed up for two of Forest's courses—English 130, the single-author course (Twain again) and English 157, a special-studies course of the student's own choice and composition.

In Special Studies, Tony, much to Forest's strained indulgence, had requested permission to study the crime novel. His performance in the Twain displayed a talent for wit and irony and even joy that Forest never found in national or international conferences devoted to wit and irony and joy in writing or reading or living.

The authors Tony had elected to read for 157 were either former investigators or cops, so there was a great deal of banter, code words, phrases that created the sights and sounds of precinct stations, local politics, inner-city adventures. Tony's term paper on the need for each community to have its own volunteer police contingent was so well written, even provocative, that Forest wondered if he ought to pursue the wispy suspicion of plagiarism.

But when Tony appeared in his office, his defense of the paper left no doubt in Forest's mind that he had written it himself. Without help. In the fourteen pages, there were six grammatical errors, two spelling errors and only one reference problem. It deserved and received an A.

When Forest returned the paper, Tony, as if unconcerned, resisted checking the grade until he reached the door. There, hand on the knob, he glanced down, opened the paper, stared at the grade for several seconds. He checked the first page to be sure his name was there. He glanced up, actually blushed, and said, "Hey, thanks, man."

"Don't thank me, Tony. Thank yourself."

E-130? The Twain course?

"So, you liked *Huck Finn*, Tony?"

"That was an important book, man."

"Important for whom? For Twain?"

"Important for us. You realize that for every black person those days there were forty, fifty, a hundred white judges made the laws for them?"

Forest waited, sure some attempt would be made to expand or enlighten.

"Every white person—man, woman, child, young or old—ruled every black person's life. That book was written a hundred years ago. Twain was way ahead of his time, man. I'll bet you no writer writing today will ever write a book as important as *Huck Finn*."

A delay of one more minute.

"You know, I know I'll never be able to write a book like that, but I'm glad I can read it like every year or two. The rest of my life. I wish I could say that to whats-is-name, Mark Twain."

⟨⟨⟩⟩

At commencement, when he marched with the other seniors down the carpet toward the stage, Tony searched among the black-gowned, tassel-capped faculty for Forest, found him, blew him a kiss. After the ceremony, at the reception for faculty, students, families, Tony brought his mother and father and two older sisters to meet Forest and Emerald.

"This," he announced to his family, "is my friend Forest Butler. Professor Forest Butler. And this is Emerald, his wife. They got me this." He brandished his rolled and beribboned diploma.

Tony's family—all four of whom had flown up from Los Angeles—had brought Professor Butler a gift. Four jars of pesto sauce.

"Made," Mrs. Coniglio said, "with my own *basilico*, Professor Butler. My grandmother's recipe. Exactly like in the old country. Best gift we can give you. It says *grazie, grazie tante*. All he talks about, Tony, he's home, is you. And you, Mrs. Butler."

Tony's father, shaking Emerald's hand: "Me and my wife never eat Japanese food. We ain't—what do you call it, Anthony?"

Tony laughed. "Sophisticated."

"Sophisticated," Mr. Coniglio said.

Lord God, Forest thought, glancing around the room, how glad I am.

Tony was one of the only students with whom Forest continued even a casual relationship after graduation. It became more than a teacher-student relationship. They were friends. Once or twice a month, they went to a cafe together for a meal. Forest invited Tony home twice for Emerald's display of at least eight different dishes and introduced him to saki. In bed after the second meal, Emerald confided to him she wished Tony were their son.

Following a year of unremarkable graduate work in communications at San Francisco State, Tony transferred to Berkeley to work with a distinguished professor of urban law, a woman praised by a variety of mayors and police chiefs and students with varying degrees of what is called a social conscience. Tony required three instead of the usual two years to earn a master's degree but the degree in criminal justice was awarded with honors.

"Yo, Forest. A master's degree. How about that? I am a Master. I da may-an!"

※

When Emerald and Maria had paid shared tributes to Forest for proving that a so-called mediocre student could be more than a mediocre human being. Paul Scarborough had to play the bad guy. Who cared? Not Maria or Emerald and not Forest.

"Training to be a cop," Paul Scarborough said, "is like training a stray dog to be a pit bull. Detective. Sounds like a Brooklyn hood talking. 'Hey, youse guys see de 'tective?'"

"The only thing you know about cops or detectives," Maria-the-expert reminded her husband, and reminding him again that she'd reminded him before, "is that they carry gats and wear gumshoes and they always ask the sergeant, 'You got fingerprints?'"

※

Three years of patrol and squad-car duty in San Francisco led Tony to Homicide, where he moved up the ladder from investigator to detective to Assistant Chief and then Chief of Unit. He was, he confided at occasional dinners at his home (pasta at every meal served by his Italian-born wife) or the Butlers' home (Japanese food every time), aiming for Chief of Detectives of the city of San Francisco.

Three years ago, a phone call: "Yo, Forest. An hour ago. I'm now Chief of Detectives. You better say sir to me, man, the next time we meet."

❦

Now, nine days after the death of Farleigh O'Brien, Anthony Coniglio sits here on Tamalpais Avenue in Berkeley sipping saki.

"That was a fantastic meal, Emerald. I haven't had sashimi like that even in Japan-town. And the tempura? I made a pig of myself. Emerald, can I ask you a question? About Japan?"

"Yes, of course. You go to Japan?"

"No, no. Just curious. Suicide. When someone in Japan commits suicide, isn't it usually with a knife? I read somewhere, or maybe I saw it in a movie, this man sitting on the floor, on a mat. He held a sword like this and then pushed it into his belly."

"Oh, yes. Very honorable way to die. Many years ago, you dishonored, you commit suicide with sword. Sometimes knife, long knife. Seppuku. Now, today, people don't often use seppuku. Sleep pills, jump from cliffs. Young people in love, students not get into best university—seppuku but not sword. Jump from bridge or tube from end of car into your mouth? It is called...?"

"Stupid," Forest offered.

"No, no. I cannot think of word. It is so long."

"So long, it's been good to know you? That's a song by Woody Guthrie."

176

Emerald: "Forest, you stop..."

"Asphyxiation?" Tony volunteered.

"Yes. As-fix...that it."

"I'd take sleeping pills," Tony says. "It's painless. Wouldn't you, Forest?"

"No. I'd spend an evening with Henry Kissinger and laugh myself to death."

"Emerald?"

"You shouldn't have asked," Forest says. "Suicide one-oh-one lecture coming up."

Emerald ignores him. "I admire writer—a hero Japan. Is very lear...lear...learned man."

"Was," Forest says.

"Is very learned man. Very disciplined. He loves..."

"Loved."

"Loves ancient culture. Believes people today weak, no discipline, no respect ancient traditions. He admire seppuku. I commit suicide, I honor my esteemed teacher and hero Mishima. Mishima almost more my hero than Forest."

"Oh, thank you, daring. I'm now second to a ghost."

"I say almost."

Tony says, "I think you're safe, Forest. No woman would cook such delicious food for a man she didn't love. But it's late. I better go. One more question. Bonnie MacNeil. But hold your answer. May I use your bathroom?"

Tony had used the downstairs bath every time he'd been here before, as had his wife, but tonight he chooses to go upstairs. Not important. While he is gone, Emerald continues her work in the kitchen, and Forest observes the fire, thinking about Bonnie O'Neil and Tony's interest in that tanned beauty he, Forest, will have to meet with soon.

When Tony returns and sits again beside his replenished little pot of saki, he says, "Bonnie MacNeil."

177

"O'Neil," Forest says.

"Sorry. When she was Bonnie O'Brien—did you know them well?"

"We were at their house," Emerald says, coming from the kitchen, "four times. They came here five times."

"We went to dinner together, at restaurants, three or four times," Forest said. "Yes, I'd say we knew them well."

"Is Bonnie a jealous woman, do you think? Did she feel he shafted her?"

"Shafted?" Emerald cocks her head, as if she might not have heard the word correctly.

"Cheated," Tony says.

"Ah, so," Emerald looks to Forest to supply the answer.

"If you think she killed her husband, her ex-husband," Forest says, "forget it. If she intended to kill him it would have been before she kicked him out of the house. She did that, you know. Kicked him out."

"Yes, I know. She told me."

Tony, on his feet, offers to help with the dishes, but Emerald insists on doing the work herself. While Tony and Forest talk in the living room. Forest hears her, when she finishes her work, go to the phone to discuss her new career with Maria Scarborough.

Tony succumbs to the offer of a cup of coffee for the road. He speaks first.

"Two sources have said O'Brien was ambidextrous, Forest. One was you, one was his former wife."

"Well, Bonnie should know."

"It was *not* suicide, Forest."

Forest swallows a large intake of gin-and-tonic, lets his hopes rise and settle so he can speak without gargling. "You're sure?"

"I'm sure."

"Who killed him?"

"Once I come up with a motive I'll be closer to the name of the killer. We still have important ballistics and lab reports to come in."

"I have a question for you."

"Shoot. I'm sorry. I mean go ahead."

"I don't know anything about guns. What was the gun?"

"A thirty-eight Special."

"Is that a big gun?"

"Bigger than a twenty-two. Smaller than a forty-five."

"Could a woman lift, I mean shoot, a thirty-eight? A really young woman. Slight. A student?"

A flick of Tony's eyes and a brief twitch of his lips too quickly controlled do not escape Forest's attention.

"Well, yeah. A forty-five would be unlikely. The recoil could break her wrist. Why? You know something I ought to know?"

"No, no. Of course not. I'll tell you the truth, Tony. I'm trying to write a novel. I guess it's a murder mystery. And I'm making the killer a young woman. Nineteen, twenty years old. So I need to know details like this. Can I call you now and then? Just for advice?"

"Hey, I've gotta read that when it comes out, man. Yeah, sure. A woman. In fact—and don't breathe a word of this to anyone yet, not even to Emerald—promise? Okay, we've found some hairs. You know we vacuum rug, furniture, bed, everything. DNA. The lab—man, modern technology is incredible. We found some hairs."

"I'll be damned. I just made up my student-killer for my novel. I had no idea there was even a female..."

"Damn clever, Forest. Maybe I ought to hire you."

"Female student. I'll be goddamned."

179

"No, you won't. But in this novel you're making up that has this female student you're making up, the victim you're making up, he-she is a college professor?"

"You got it."

"You've got a keen imagination, Professor. Scary keen."

"I'll tell you one thing, Tony. That hair you found?"

"Hairs."

"Those hairs, they couldn't be from Mary Beth Lederberg. I think she's dying."

"I know she is."

"You know?"

"Yeah. Too bad." He glances at his watch, jerks his body. "Hey, man, I have to run. Thank Emerald for me. Let's get together in San Francisco."

"Definitely. Soon. But if I get stuck can I call?"

"Anytime, man. Day or night. But remember. Not a word to anyone. Not even Emerald. You know how women..."

"You have my word, Detective Coniglio."

"Later, man."

⸎

Forest returns to his study, stares at the computer. Tonight, fellow, you are going to be surprised.

Emerald, behind him: "I'm sorry I not say good-night to Tony. He leave so soon."

"No problem, Emmy. Not the slightest even most miniscule problem. He praised..."

"Miniscool?"

"A tiny school."

"Forest, if I aren't so happy I be angry." She goes to the antique oak dictionary stand and begins to leaf through the pages of the large Merriam Webster. "How you spell mini...?"

"My dear, it means tiny. Tinier than tiny."

She closes the dictionary, victorious. "I like Tony much much much. Tony tells the truth."

"Truth?"

"He said my sashimi better than sashimi Japan-town."

"Tony is famous far and wide for his truthfulness. He'll have to change, or he won't ever be able to run for president of the United States."

"He talk about Farreigh suicide?"

"Not at all. Well, yes, he said it was unfortunate."

"Unfortunate not word Tony use."

"Oooh, very perceptive, dear author. Okay, that's *my* word. Tony said, let's see, he said, 'Too bad.'"

"Yes, Tony say, 'Too bad.' You see? I will be a writer."

"Emerald, my little gem, I do believe you will make a very impressive writer. To fit appropriate language to a character is the second major rule of writing a novel."

"The first rule?"

"Excuse me?"

"Ranaguage to character second rue. First major rue. Tell me first major rue?"

"Oh. The first major rule, my little delicacy, is to put your edible ass on a chair and start writing."

"Ediboorass?" And Emerald, eyes wide, rushes to the Merriam Webster dictionary. As she flips the pages she sings: "Two week...I free in two week...I write novera two week..."

CHAPTER 11

Providence. That's what it is. Who would believe such a stroke of luck, such a trick of fate, such smiling fortune? Were Forest to have completed the novel and, in Chapter 8 or 9, suddenly, without preparing the reader, introduced the character Tony and his offer of information such as Tony in real life provided, every editor would return the manuscript collect, not even taking time to insert a form rejection slip.

Do such windfalls—pieces of important evidence dropping into the lap of the all but hopeless detective, evidence proving the guilt or innocence of a suspect—do such windfalls occur in real criminal investigations?

It doesn't matter. This—writing a novel—is not dependent on so-called real life. Don't, insists the old adage, look a gift horse in the mouth, Forest.

What, the professor in him wonders, could have been the origin of that little piece of folk wisdom? It had to be related to the age of a horse being gauged by the condition of its teeth. No matter how worn the teeth and thus how old the animal, the damned horse, a gift and therefore free, should be accepted without cute demurrals. Tony has been, will remain, a gift horse.

He—Forest the writer, not Forest the professor—will be talking to Tony again. He will have to. Even as he knows there might be other relevant details coming as gifts, a sharp little tooth of failure bites at his skin. He whips his head about, fully expecting a black widow spider or a rabid bat poised to bite again.

What if Farleigh O'Brien had been killed? What if Tony tracked down the killer? What if...? What if...?

No matter those or any other what-ifs. He has found a way to tell the novel he intends to write. This, the third novel, will be a winner. He not just feels it, he knows it.

He will now write straight on, day and night. He will not think about research papers and lectures and classes and students. When his sabbatical ends and he is scheduled to return to classes, he will, if necessary, request a semester off without pay to complete the work. Unable now to even hope for another sabbatical for another six or seven years, he will buy a semester of freedom. The cost? Fifty-five thou, give or take. But how better spend a piece of his (their, his and Emerald's) savings?

Consider your fortune, your good fortune, Forest. Two gift horses have galloped into your life in less than twenty-four hours: Tony the first, last night, and second, just this afternoon, Paul Scarborough.

~⪘~

Paul's call had come in the late afternoon.

"Forest, I'm just leaving the campus. I have a tape from one of my students. She recorded it last night. Glenn in the communications department made a copy for me. It might just help you get a grip on what drives...drove...the great Irish fart-laureate. I'll drop it off on the way home."

The doorbell rang twenty-five minutes later, at 5:40. Like a practiced marathoner, Paul handed off the cassette ("Call me tonight, tell me what you think.") and raced back to his car, certain, probably, that a hurried departure would drive Forest to the tape even faster.

In fact, Forest was closing the door of his study and fitting the cassette in place before Paul's car left the curb. He played it immediately, and now he plays it again, not for the second but for the third time.

⤳

Music (not rock but something loud and twangy and what would certainly be called cool) begins and fades.

Woman's voice: Hello. This is *New Breezes* and I'm Dierdre O'Connel. Some years ago, more than I care to admit, I was a student at Sarah Lawrence College. I decided to follow the recommendations of many of my friends and sign up for a course with a young, terribly bright poet named Farleigh O'Brien.

My friends were correct. Farleigh O'Brien was the most exciting, brightest, most talented professor I'd had in six years of college. I later directed many of my close friends to his classes.

O'Brien went on to teach at Harvard and Indiana. He is now a tenured full professor at Saint Catherine's, a small liberal arts college in the Bay Area in California. He has won just about every honor a poet can hope for in this country, including two Guggenheims, two National Arts Endowment grants, the National Book Award and the Pulitzer Prize. He has also won several honors in Europe. O'Brien, in his mid-forties, has twice been nominated for the Nobel Prize.

Farleigh O'Brien is my guest today on *New Breezes*. Farleigh, a question. You have published three books of poetry and a volume of essays, and I don't believe you have received a single line of criticism about your work. Does that disturb you? Are you on the edge of your chair, waiting to be smitten?

Farleigh: (Chuckles.) You mean anticipating? No. But I have had reactions that could not be called praise. I meet with a group of poets once a month. These are established well-published people I respect and admire. They can be very tough. I wince, sitting here, remembering some of their comments about my work.

DO: Do you have to fight smugness, self-satisfaction? All those honors. Those nominations for the Nobel Prize. You've published three books of poetry. When you think of the number of volumes of poetry and critical essays and plays written by poets like Sachs and Cardinale and other poets who've won the Nobel, you can't help but be flattered.

Farleigh: Oh, don't misunderstand. I am flattered. But what can I say without appearing pretentiously humble? Awards, honors, recognition don't impress me. Some pretty awful poets have won the Nobel Prize, as, I suspect, have some pretty miserable economists and physicists. You know, there is a Zen comment that I have pasted on the door of my room: "Fame is a flower that dries in the rain." Wallace Stevens pleaded with committees and foundations not to reward him. I would be writing poetry now even if I'd never have another poem published.

DO: Would you please read a poem from your new collection *Love's Doors and Other Limits*.

Farleigh: Sure. Let's see. This one is about a summer day when my daughter was nine. She was preparing for a fishing trip we were taking the next day. She

186

was checking her tackle box. She cried out. I ran to
her. A fish hook had gone into the palm of her
hand. The title is "Summer Day."

> At noon the beast
> of the noonday sun
> stretches out on the roof
> of our house.
> I sit on the porch in shade.
> Six white grapes in a blue bowl
> wait to be eaten.
> Li Po and his second wife,
> both bent with age,
> traveled to the mountains
> on the hottest day of summer
> and dipped mint leaves
> into the cold waters
> of the spring
> where
> in the last days
> of summer
> the goddess of Winter Nights
> bathes with the God
> of the Black Swans.
> She cools him
> with her frosted lips.
> At my side iced tea
> lemon yellow
> in the white pitcher with
> a chipped rim
> offers sugar citrus scent
> into the air.
> A sprinkler carves water
> out of the breeze
> to green the lawn.
> I lie back
> and close my eyes
> and Robert Cohen and Brett

settle in my lap.
The planet moves
through space.
When you scream
my heart
twists in my chest
and I leap awake.
The No. 5 hook
designed to pull a stickleback
free of river shadows
is a black red metal line
under the skin of your palm.
Your eyes spill tears
of protest
at this cruel attack.
In my arms the taste
of your salt
and the heave of your
small smooth chest
stuffs my heart
with the sorrow
I would feel
were I the finned father
swimming
through the river shadows
as the mouth
of my daughter
is ripped
and she is reeled
away from me
forever
through the water roof
of home
and is drawn
up into
the lethal summer air.

DO: That is so beautiful. That is really a California poem. It just could not be New Mexico or Vermont or Kansas or Warsaw. Oh, it is just so beautiful.

Farleigh: Thank you. It still hurts, the memory of my daughter's pain and outrage that day. Just now, as I read it to you, I wonder about the word *lethal*. It doesn't fit. Something less human, more fishy. (Laughter.) Then again, why not? The air will kill the daughter fish. It *is* lethal. I think I'll leave it. It feels right. Poetry should make the reader as well as the poet feel.

DO: You are such a gentle man, so calm. And so profound. I remember you in class—okay, it was fifteen years ago—never upset, always concerned about your students, always filled with a tenderness that made us all, men and women, really, well, humbled. Now you're famous, and your poetry still has that effect.

Do you ever feel anger? Ever? Do you ever feel mean? Your romantic poetry, your political poetry, have no bravado. Each poem, each line, is pure beatitude. I think you speak to the best in all of us. That must be why you're so loved and admired. You deserve—

Farleigh: Please, please. You make me sound like Mother Theresa.

DO: Would you read one more poem? We have maybe two minutes left. How about my favorite? Page seven, your first book. "The Last Four Queen Anne Cherries."

Farleigh: I like that one, too. Okay. Another California poem. "The Last Four Queen Anne Cherries." It's one paragraph, structured as prose.

> I know the cherries will be ripe today,
> and so I come at noon to pick enough

for three pies, one of which I will take to my neighbor who often leaves in my refrigerator a salmon or a sea bass he has caught that day at the bay. I had forgotten about the grosbeaks. They know not just to the day but to the hour when my Queen Anne cherries reach perfection. Between dawn and this moment they have eaten every cherry except the four which hang in one tight cluster near the center of the tree. I do not have the heart to pick them. I try to shake my empty fist at the two birds that fly from behind the redwood trees onto that one branch and that one stem and that last single cluster. I cannot watch. I turn away, trying to be angry. As I walk back to my kitchen I want to shout out, "Damn grosbeaks," but I only groan. The birds lift their brown speckled bodies into the redwood tree, depositing a final payment of one fallen feather. Then, ah, a second.

DO: Oh, my. Lovely. Just lovely. The impulse is to say you're a California poet, but your visions are universal. Ginzberg or Stafford, someone, I forget now, told me you were the first to write these short narrative paragraphs of poetry.

Farleigh: Your informants are too generous. The Old Testament preceded me by approximately two thousand years.

DO: Farleigh O'Brien, thank you so much. My guest has been the deservedly famous poet, Farleigh O'Brien. Thank you, Farleigh.

Farleigh: Thank *you*, Dierdre. It was fun.

⌒≋⌒

Forest has to grip his right hand with his left to keep the phone from shaking when he calls Paul. Maria answers, says she will get The Master, who is waiting with breath a-baited with gin.

Forest knows, as if the odor of Paul's breath comes through the plastic receiver, that Paul has downed several more than the usual two or three pre-supper martinis.

"I'm awaiting," Paul says, "breath abated."

"The man," Forest says, "could charm the Texas chainsaw murderer into planting posies and writing verses for children."

"He was the Prince of Peace, wasn't he, Forest? No one will believe he could carve your heart out with a dull bread knife. Was this the face that lunched on a thousand slips? No one will believe he's capable—excuse me, was capable—of raping Grandma Moses and stealing her paintbrushes. We, *Sie und Ich*, can only shut up and accept his successes. He could have been President of the United States. One smile and one saintly sigh and one sonnet and he'd carry every state in the Onion. Certainly a hundred percent of the women's vote."

"The student who gave you the tape," Forest asks. "Was she ga-ga?"

"Of course. The very best student I've had since Maria, and she'd give herself along with her three sisters and her mother to O'Brien for breakfast and then thank him for his generosity. You better get on with that goddamn novel, fella. No more planning. No more theorizing. No more distractions. Put your ass on the stool and type away! Damn but I envy you."

⌒≋⌒

Sitting in his chair, staring into the blank and thirsty screen of his computer, Forest blows out a lungful of

191

air, like a sprinter about to leave the block, and he does indeed write. He writes without concern for syntax or grammar or spelling. Just pour it out, man. Pour...it...out!

Though he calls this first piece Chapter 1—typed, promptly, right there at the top of the page, he knows that whatever he is now throwing onto the screen might very well end up as chapter six. Or ten. Or it might, before the final rewrite, be totally purged. Names, dates, time might be, probably will be, altered to offend the guilty. But here he comes.

Here I come, Random House!

Or will it be Harper?

Hadn't it been the Harper editor who was the most positive with the two last novels ("Actually, Professor Butler, though we reject this manuscript we would very much like to see more of your work. The talent is there.")

Harper it will be.

Farleigh O'Brien, you bastard, finally! Forest feels like John Wayne rushing across a verbal no-man's land, assaulting a bunker full of poets.

～⚜～

Friday, March 26th, 1993

Nine days after the death of O'Brien.

> Who killed Clancy Cavanaugh? Not me, though I have to admit I'm not sorry he's dead. Cavanaugh was buried, I hear, in his cowboy boots. Mercifully, his stetson was forgotten.

～⚜～

After two hours of non-stop typing Forest rolls his chair back on the mat of slick plywood. Enough.

As the pages slide from his printer, he paces the floor, returning to count the pages by hand, not bothering to check the numbers on the upper corner of each sheet but calling each number aloud as the paper appears. He needs not to just see the pages, he must feel them. 1...2...3...4...

"Eighteen." Eighteen pages of Chapter One of my novel *Murder by Metaphor*. He will go on immediately to chapter two and page nineteen, but the small of his back is warning him: Rest, Forest, relax. Restore energy.

Standing at the west window of the living room, he scans the Berkeley hillside falling away to the flatlands. Just enough light remains to wash the Golden Gate Bridge with the dusky rose of an autumn evening. Lights blink on-off-on in the San Francisco office buildings across the bay. In the middle of the gray-black spans of metal that compose the Oakland Bay Bridge, red taillights inchworm southwest from Berkeley and Oakland. Headlights glare north, out of San Francisco, toward Berkeley and Oakland. The battling lights merge, fight, part, merge, neither side winning, neither losing, neither side surrendering.

Emerald is on her way home. She will arrive in— he checks his watch—a half-hour. Nine more days of the traffic battles on the Bay Bridge, and she will be home every day all day.

She will be writing her "noveru."

Forest mixes a gin-and-tonic and sits on the sofa where one drink creates memories, two drinks create related memories.

CHAPTER 12

They rented a house on Josephine Street in the Berkeley flats the first three years of their marriage, but the day after Forest published his book on Twain and Faulkner (title: *Two Southerners With But A Single Spirit*, Yale Press) he—they—had bought this house in the Berkeley hills.

The evening of their first day here, Emerald had been giddy, hauling clothes and records from the car, chattering in portions of Japanese and then English. Forest stumbled among the crates and boxes and suitcases, singing odds and ends of arias from *Aida*, *Barbiere de Seville*, *Lucia*, clearing a space for the large varnished door that would serve as desk for his Olivetti and academic paraphernalia.

Emerald, too exhausted and too frenetic to go out, had convinced him to have a pizza delivered. Pizza, the food she had taken to within minutes after she'd arrived from Kyoto. She surveyed each slice before biting into it, selecting the precise area that promised sausage or green pepper or mushroom.

They sat on the sofa, eating pizza, drinking beer, laughing, talking. Ideas tumbled and rattled about like marbles released from a bag tacked to the ceiling.

Then, with a sudden flood of tears, Emerald was bemoaning the plight of her lonely parents. Forest urged her to invite them to visit, to stay for as long as they wished. As soon as they had the house in order. There were two large extra bedrooms that could be painted and filled with suitable furniture in three or four weeks.

"Invite them, Emmy. I want to meet the in-laws. After all, they're your laws."

Emerald, after the fifth slice of pizza and third glass of white wine, had pushed crates and suitcases aside, reciting Yokasaki as she unbuttoned Forest's shirt and trousers and lay back on the polished oak floor in front of their very first fire in the stone fireplace, and pulled him down upon and into her. She translated Yokasaki's verses into hesitant but softly whispered singsong English. Forest groaned as he felt himself sucked deeper and deeper inside the love of his life.

> Your thighs flutter
> like butterfly wings
> Two pink doves
> suck your breasts
> I cling to your shoulders
> and pull you across the grass
> into the lake
> Seven carp
> Come to drink
> your juices.

To welcome Emerald home from San Francisco Forest opens a bottle of Stag's Leap Chardonnay. He'd bought a case of the expensive wine two years ago, the day his article on Twain's last bitter years had been published by *New York Review of Books.* Three bottles remain after this one.

Forest insists they have dinner at Chez Panisse to celebrate their love and her coming freedom, but she has brought food from San Francisco's Japan-town. They sit at the table, Forest exuberant, Emerald exuberant.

"Do you remember our first night in this house, Emmy?"

"Of course I do. Yokasaki. White thighs on blue iris petals. " She reaches her hands across the table, and he catches them in his own.

"I'm going to write tonight," he says.

"I, too. That why I bring food and not make food."

"Work on your novel?"

"Yes. Every minute aru day nothing in my head but noveru noveru noveru. It will be very important noveru. For me for you."

When she lowers her cheek onto his hands she is crying.

She goes to her private computer in her private study at 7:05. For the first time in years, Forest cleans up the meal's aftermath. He goes to his private computer in his private study. It is seven-thirty.

At nine o'clock, Emerald almost staggers to bed and falls immediately into a deep sleep.

By nine, when Emerald drops into her bed without even brushing her teeth Forest is on page six of Chapter 2. At eleven, he, too, staggers into the bedroom. Emmy is under the blankets, sleeping.

He does not shower, does not brush his teeth. He stays awake long enough to remove his clothes, slides beneath the blankets naked, drops off to sleep immediately.

At the sound of his first light snore, Emerald sits up, leaves the bed, draws her magenta robe around her body, pulls the blankets close about Forest's na-ked shoulders, leaves the room. Seated at her private desk she writes for an hour, stopping now and then to wipe her eyes.

Forest dreams.

A bell or whistle—Forest cannot identify which—interrupts a ten-year-old Forest Butler's observation of his mother at the kitchen stove. Forest the child, sitting at the table, hears the last gasps of steam whis-tling up through the throat of the pot. Ten-year-old Forest's mother, at the stove, pours two heaping spoons of instant coffee into a red mug and fills it with water. She is talking to someone in another room. Is the voice from the other room his father's voice, his sister Angeline's?

"Forest, is for you."

The words, singly or together, make no sense.

"What's for me, Momma?"

"Terephone. Mary Beth friend, Jeanne."

The dream, in the process of fading away, carries off his mother, carries off the kitchen, the steaming coffee. Forest is awake, here in his bed in Berkeley. Emerald, in her magenta robe, is nudging his shoul-der.

"Mary Beth?"

"Mary Beth friend, Jeanne. She cries."

When Forest accepts the phone with his left hand he sees, on the clock on the bedside table, that it is not quite three o'clock. Rain thuds on the roof, washes across the bedroom windows. This, he knows, has to be bad news.

"Jeanne. Is something wrong?"

"Mary Beth wants you to come over as soon as you can. She's sick, she's so...oh, there's the doorbell. It's the doctor."

"I'll be right there."

With the cold wind and stinging rain and the empty autumn streets, the possibility of the arrival of good will or comfort or hope is less than zero. On such a night as this dogs howl on the fogged Welsh moors; at the coast low-slung cars filled with teenagers speed through fences and drop over cliffs; murderers with knives in hand prowl the hallways of homes of lonely widows who, asleep in their rocking chairs in front of meager fires, place their trust in God and Schlage Locks Inc.

Jeanne must have been watching for him. She opens the door before he reaches the steps; and she falls into his arms, weeping, making a valiant but failed effort to control herself, to talk coherently. She ends up taking his hand and leading him upstairs, where a dark-bearded bear of a man in a mountain jacket is bending over Mary Beth. His large arm, behind her, supports her in a partly upright position. With his free hand, he moves the cup of the stethoscope from neck to shoulder to lower back to mid-back. She tries valiantly to respond to his request that she cough.

After collecting sufficient strength to twice expel a sound that is no more than a grunt, her body follows his arm down into her pillow.

"Forest?"

"I'm here, Mary Beth."

The doctor growls, "Just a minute," to no one in particular, and reaches beneath the blankets with rubber-gloved hands to press here and there, to nod at her moans, to observe her face, to murmur questions in a voice filled with gruff concern. When he draws his arm free and brings the blankets up to her chin, Mary Beth seems so small, so weightless, that were he to release her she would float up out of her bed like a helium-filled balloon.

But instead of rising she sinks deeper, until, her large, slightly bulging eyes bright and moist, she resembles one of those waifs out of a sentimental Victorian novel destined to suffer a series of miseries before being saved and anointed and admitted into royalty.

Mary Beth is not going to be saved. Not tonight.

Unlike the last time Forest visited, when he'd interviewed her, Mary Beth's face is empty of makeup. Against her cotton skin the blue-black smudges, like a small squad of thin, flat leaches, seem to be dining on her throat and cheeks. Too weak to move her head, she rolls her eyes so she might see Forest better.

"I must tell you before I leave."

Jeanne, behind him, says, "She's going to the hospital."

The word *hospital* is muffled in sobs. It seems somehow unreasonable for such a sturdy sun-browned peasant-woman to submit so uncontrollably to tears.

"Forest."

"Yes, Mary Beth. Can I do something?"

"I've called the ambulance," the doctor says, as if talking only to Mary Beth. "It should be here in a few minutes." He turns to Jeanne. "You'd better put a few things in a bag. I'll be at the hospital when you get there." He leaves the room without so much as a nod in Forest's direction.

Forest hears the door close downstairs. He wonders if it might be inappropriate to sit on the bed. Or on the chair. He remains standing. Closer to her now, he is aware of the scent. Where did he know it before? Ah, the depths of the caves into which he'd descended once during a childhood vacation in Kentucky. Mammoth Caves, Kentucky. The scent of bats, of guano.

"I don't want you at the hospital, Forest. But I want you to know something. Important."

The words come in bunches of two and three, preceded and followed by shallow, labored breathing.

"Can it wait, Mary Beth? You need your strength."

"I'm dying, Forest."

He wants to deny it, to assure her she is imagining it, but he knows she'd not permit such cheap deceit. When he takes her hand her fingers move slightly inside his, as if they are trying to tap out the secret code that will make everything intelligible.

"I have AIDS. I gave it to Farleigh. I knew I had it. This is not a deathbed appeal for salvation. So-called cultured men used to require cognac and a cigar after dinner. For the next hundred years, at least, so-called cultured women will have to require revenge. I gained my revenge, didn't I?

"So, here you are, Forest. Scholars don't usually get such important information until it's too late. I wanted to be sure you knew the details before they became rumors that could never be substantiated. Jeanne...we've not been sexually intimate for years. She's been checked. So far so good." She closes her eyes and spills out a thin, vaporous giggle. "I was about to say I'd die if I gave Jeanne AIDS."

"Mary Beth, is there anyone...?"

She moves her head from side to side. "My family is scattered. Everything, not much, goes to Jeanne...she's been...my alter ego. She's strong. If we had met early on..."

Forest, with his forefinger, wipes away the tears that appear on her lower eyelids. He brushes her hair from her forehead.

"Been a good friend." He thinks she means Jeanne until she adds, "Only one in the department. Jeanne has papers. Use them. You wish, use my name. I'll be called things...but won't matter now."

From the doorway, Jeanne says what sounds like, "The ambulance is here, Mary Beth," but most of the syllables are lost in sobs. She steps aside for the three paramedics, two men and a woman. All three wear masks and rubber gloves. They carry a steel stretcher that unfolds into a gurney.

"Better leave, Forest."

"Can I kiss you, Mary Beth?"

"Sure you want to?" The chuckle this time is thinner than vapor.

"I'm sure, my dear."

He kisses her on her hot dry lips and then on both cheeks, feeling not at all frightened. He wishes with sincere anguish that he had been more attentive to this woman over the years, had spent more time with her, had demonstrated before this moment, before tonight, his appreciation of her perception of him as her friend.

"The ambulance," Jeanne says.

He makes room for the paramedics, but when they try to open the stretcher the space between bed and wall is too narrow.

"We'll have to carry her downstairs. We'll put her on the gurney down there."

Jeanne sweeps in front of them. In one movement, she tucks the blankets about Mary Beth's withered body and lifts her lovingly into her arms. She precedes the medics down the stairs, her cheek against Mary Beth's lips.

The ambulance—medics and Mary Beth inside—drives off, red lights blinking. Forest, on the porch, embraces Jeanne and whispers a request that she call him as soon as possible. She nods into his shoulder while she presses a large bulky manuscript envelope into his hand.

Perhaps it is the new and more ferocious sweep of rain, perhaps it is the warmth of the heater, the swish-swash of the wiper blades. Perhaps it is a simple overdose of sadness. For whatever reason, Forest chooses not to turn up Eucalyptus Road on his return from Mary Beth's home but to continue down Cedar to San Pablo and north on San Pablo to

University. The car, with a will of its own, makes its way toward the bay, finds the pier, edges forward.

He stops, turns off the engine. Waits inside the car, warm, dry, his rain jacket open. He wants to close his eyes and drift into sleep, but he is too fiercely awake.

Tilting his seat back, he watches an oil tanker carry its stringed-bead lights out toward the Golden Gate Bridge, which is not visible but which lies over there to the front and right, defying the rain. He thinks of Conrad. Boats. Strong and troubled men. Ripe exotic South Sea bays and jungles. *Victory. Heart of Darkness. Lord Jim.* Coppola had ruined *Heart of Darkness* for him. He'd never think of Kurtz again without seeing a bloated Brando and the monstrously bloated film. Coppola, with the aplomb of a swallower of lime Jell-O, had executed not Kurtz but Conrad.

Edward G. Robinson. Captain Larson. *The Sea Wolf.* Jack London—the best and the worst. London, our American Gorki. Why hadn't Forest Butler led the life of Jack London? Or B. Traven, that weird and defiant exile who made Fitzgerald and Hemingway and Stein look like meringue baby dolls.

Conrad, London, Traven—they all lived through adventures that slid out of their minds onto pages. They'd had no need to make up stories or characters or landscapes. They did not have to pretend they were someone investigating, exploiting, the lives and deaths of other better men. They had drained their fiction out of the reservoirs of their own lives.

Forest's life has had no such adventures. His flat feet and his vision ("My God!" the doctor had yelped. "Can you see the wall the chart's on?") and his heart (which had quite surprisingly dropped its murmur to a whisper in his thirties and to complete silence in his forties) had kept him out of the army after WWII and, as well, the Korean War, in which, as in the late forties, he'd tried unsuccessfully to enlist. Flatter feet. Worse vision. The murmur? Revived a year or so ago. Was that (his own orchestrated safety) why he never found it possible to discuss Paul's experiences in combat? *But I did try to get in, Paul. I tried, damn it. They wouldn't take me. I tried, Paul. I'm not a coward, Paul.*

He had not said that, will not say that.

The car is colder now. Forest starts the motor so he might use the heater. The wiper blades, not having been turned off earlier, start swish-swashing again. Through the clear arcs of glass he sees, ahead, in the water, ten feet below, the final length of the floating pier extending out over the water for ten or fifteen yards. In the wash of the tanker, the pier bobs up and down.

He and Emerald had come here several times their first year together. She would close her eyes to intensify the rhythmic rise and fall, and one night she admitted that once, as a little girl, she had wanted to be in the Japanese navy. She had wanted to command two or three hundred men and lead them into battle against a flotilla of enemy—yes, the enemy had probably been American—cruisers and aircraft carriers and battleships.

Somehow, though Japanese as well as American ships were controlled by advanced technology, and in spite of the fact that Japan was not permitted to have a warrior navy, somehow, Emerald had seen herself as a Japanese Joan of Arc standing at the bow of a carrier, a shining steel cutlass in her hand.

"Charge!" she screams at her warriors. Her ship moves forward into the heart of the enemy fleet. "Charge!" she screams. "Charge! Banzai!"

That night on the floating pier, replaying her fantasy, appreciating her own comic audacity, she had leaped about, shouting across the bay at the moonlit city of San Francisco: "Charge! Charge!

204

Banzai!" Like an ebullient schoolgirl, she had pranced about the pier and then had leaped, to perform a perfect swan dive into the arms of her American lover-husband.

My Emerald. My precious Emerald.

Forest, turning off the wipers, rejoices in the memory, and yearns to have Emerald in his arms at this moment. Oh, lordy, lordy, how he loves the glorious gift of that woman.

He yearns then to do something rash, something dangerous. He wants to taste the wind and the salt air, and the thrill that has evaded him all his life. He wants to completely alter the shape and drift of his life. *I will be a better man. Not for myself alone but for my beloved Emerald.*

Opening the car door, he steps out into the rain. He zips up his rain jacket, steps onto the pier. The waves and the wind charge him like an avenging enemy.

He has trouble keeping his balance but continues forward until he reaches the chain at the end of the pier. Clinging to it, he spreads his legs and braces against the wind, against the lift and fall of the platform. What if the ropes or chains or cables that anchor pier to land broke now, and the pier, a raft then, with him aboard, drifted out beneath the bridge and into the Pacific Ocean? What if he died now?

Oh, God! No! To leave his love, his Emerald, is impossible. He turns away from the lights of San Francisco to face the scattered lights of Berkeley. He will return to reclaim his goddess, his Emerald.

He charges across the pier to his car. He is alive, not, like Farleigh, dead, not, like Mary Beth, dying.

As he opens the door of his car, he pauses. The face of Mary Beth hovers there behind the steering wheel, levitating. He knows, he just simply knows for certain, that Mary Beth Lederberg is at this very moment breathing her last. Her hopes, her dreams, all those years of study, those hours and weeks and years of research and writing, everything, everything is finished. Is lost. Soon to be, if not already, forgotten.

Mary Beth Lederberg might just as well never have lived.

Forest hears his teeth chattering. Inside the car, the heater sending waves of warmth over him, he takes a deep breath, shifts the gears, drives up University and over to and up up up Tamalpais Avenue. He enters his house and climbs the stairs without turning on any lights. He is still shivering.

Removing his clothes, he hurries into a pair of flannel pajamas and a heavy sweatsuit and his thick white robe and crawls beneath the blankets beside his sleeping Emmy.

Sleep? No. Not now, not yet.

He has something that must be done this very moment.

Out of bed, still wearing sweatsuit and robe, he moves through the darkness and into his study. After closing the door he turns on the lamp. Sitting in front of the computer, he calls up a new file, types in c-h-a-p-t-e-r and the number two, and he waits.

Nothing comes.

Don't fret. Don't panic. Write. Just write. Write anything. That conversation with Paul two nights ago.

"Paul, did you ever talk to Maria about Farleigh and your brother?"

"No."

"Why not?"

"He was my brother. I loved him. Maria wouldn't believe that I loved anyone. I certainly loved my brother."

"Korea?"

"What about Korea? Did I talk to her about Korea? A bit. Please, Forest. Don't go any farther with this. Please."

He waits, staring at *Please*.

Nothing.

He waits.

Nothing more?

He types *Paul*.

Nothing. He types *Scarborough*.

And then, on the screen, the words *the silver star*.

The Silver Star for gallantry in action.

In the Korean war.

Purple Heart.

Two Purple Hearts.

Paul and I have been the closest of friends and colleagues, we have been closer than I have ever been with my brother. We...

And now Forest is typing. Not typing but writing.

...have been close friends and colleagues for thirty years. We have shared intimate secrets. I even confided...

And there it comes. There it is. Here it is. On the page...

∽

"Emerald's new attitude toward sex. Suddenly, Paul, it's different now.

"Different? What do you mean different?"

"She won't let me enter her."

"Welcome to a very exclusive club. Membership, apparently, two. Both of them men."

"You, too?"

"You got it," Paul placed his glass—his fifth martini—on the table. "Or rather, you aren't getting it. Nor am I. I don't know, Forest. But I'm not too concerned because I'm less driven than I used to be. It's no shock to the system or the psyche anymore to go for three or four weeks sans sex."

"Oh, Emerald will help me. Whenever I need it. But it's not the same. It's not the old shared love. For

Chrissake, I'm beginning to talk Marin psychobabble. Shared love, for Chrissake. Well, we'll work it out."

"Emerald will help you? I guess Maria would, if I wanted her to. But the distance between us has grown wider over the years. I'm a bastard—"

"Come on, Paul."

"I am. Not in your eyes. You indulge me to an indecent degree. In a sense, we're one person, you and I. Each of us admires the other because the one contains important elements the other needs."

"Huh? As my students respond, when I say, 'And who is Ernest Hemingway? Or Sigmund Freud? Eugene O'Neill? Mark Twain? Huh?" Paul laughs his way into a thick rasping cough. Then, under control, he pours himself a sixth or perhaps seventh martini. "I'm trying to be a better husband. I need Maria's sharp tongue and steel-trap mind. I need her desperately. She's still almost twenty years younger than I am, you know. Odd, how arithmetic works. It's undeniable truth. She was twenty years younger when we met, and she's still twenty years younger."

"Emerald's still twenty years younger than I am. Well, so we two ideal men fight exactly the same less-than-ideal frustrations. Do we share the same fates, Paul?"

"Doubt it, Forest. I'm going to Hell. Tell me, you think they talk to each other the way we do? Are they as honest with each other as we are?"

"I wonder. They are certainly very close. And to the new feminist psycho-historians, women, even if they're strangers, share intimacies with each other they'd never share with husbands or lovers."

"Can you see it? Or hear it? The dialogue? Listen to them." And Paul narrates the imagined dialogue. "Maria: Well, it's been five months now. And I still haven't let him inside me.

208

"Emerald: Three months. Shall we break our promise to each other?

"Maria: Okay. On Christmas Eve. We'll both give in.

"Emerald: (hear her little giggle.) Christmas Eve. And then? Okay after that?

"Maria: Okay after that. We've punished the bastards enough. But Paul has been patient. He's never forced it.

"Emerald: Oh, Forest, too. Never force.

"Maria: Paul doesn't need it, apparently.

"Emerald: Forest could do it every night. And next morning. Me, too. You?

"Maria: Definitely. I guess I'll reward Paul. Give him a jump-start. Get him going again. Recharge his batteries.

"Emerald: Batteries? Paul uses batteries? You use dildo?"

Forest ponders those words, and before he can ask for a clarification, Paul says, "Poetry. At least you have written poetry. You have even—okay, it was several centuries ago but you have published poetry. Why don't you write poetry anymore? Because we now have O'Brien, the American master-baiter with us?"

"No. Well, goddamn it, yes. Partly. Mostly. I hate him for that more than for any other reason I can imagine. He's destroyed one of my oldest and dearest pleasures."

Paul spends too much time cleaning up the spilled martini. When he speaks, he sharpens the edges of his words and the spaces between them, so he does not betray the fact that he is very drunk.

"Farleigh O'Brien has destroyed one of my pleasures as well. And I hate him for that."

"Your pleasures?"

"Pleasure. Singular." He waves his hand a bit, as if hoping to dismiss the subject. "Ah, Maria's home.

209

Will you join us for supper? You can call Emerald, and she can drive over here. Or maybe we can meet at a restaurant. Haven't been to Olivetto for months."

"Thanks, Paul. Better not. I'm really moving on this book."

"Are you working at all on academic stuff? Faulkner? Twain?"

"No, I haven't looked at that stuff for days."

"Christ, you're still the ambitious young graduate student seeking new intellectual conquests. I've given up. As I have on most things. Guess it's in the genes."

"Graduate student, no. Ambitious, no. Young, definitely not. Remember, I retire in five years. Conquests? None left. Genes? The only thing of interest in my jeans is my cock, and there the skin is drying up. Beginning to crack, in fact."

Paul nods, his mind, or his memory, provoked.

"There was a kid from Arkansas in my outfit in Korea. Excellent soldier. Almost illiterate. Didn't speak more than two, three words a day. When he did, they were gems. Lieutenant McCormack—graduated magna cum laude from Boston College—stuck it to him every chance he got.

"One day, the lieutenant asked this hillbilly, in front of everyone, 'Gettin' any, Keene?' And Keene—no one expecting him to say a word—says, 'Oh, just enough to keep the skin from crackin', Lootenant.'"

And something off in the distance, like a ghostly replay of an artillery barrage, catches and holds Paul's attention. He breaks into tears. Into sobs. Suddenly. Loudly. Uncontrollably.

"Fuckin' war," he says.

When Forest rises from his chair and approaches he is waved aside. He persists. He gives Paul's head a bear-hug.

"See you tomorrow. Take care, friend."

❧

Forest, barely able to keep his eyes open, finds the bed. He crawls beneath the blankets without removing either robe or sweats or pajamas. He sleeps fitfully for perhaps an hour and then he awakens to see the light on in his study. He pulls himself out of the warmth, returns to the study intending only to switch off the lamp, but instead he drops onto his chair and turns on the computer. This time he calls up his journal.

3/28/93. Left Mary Beth's house late last night trying to comprehend the magnitude of the new information. She'd given Farleigh AIDS. Or HIV, which would probably have advanced to AIDS. When had she done it? How long ago? Before she'd met Jeanne? Before Jeanne had moved in? Had he already had AIDS? If he had it and he knew it, he could have, very likely would have, killed himself.

That stops in its tracks the presumption that someone else killed him. In that case, there is no book. No no no. He could have AIDS and still been killed by someone else. Someone he'd given AIDS?

But remember! What *did* happen is of no consequence now. I'm writing a novel. I'm not recording what truly happened, I am recording what could have happened. Not recording, damn it. Imagining. Creating. I could give him AIDS. I mean, I could select any damn character I wish to have the goddamn disease and pass it on to that bastard O'Brien. I mean Cavanaugh.

⟜⟞

Forest awakens when his head falls forward to slam the keyboard. He turns off the lamp, closes the door, returns to the bed, kisses the cheek of his beautiful Emmy.

CHAPTER 13

4 a.m Saturday
March 29

Emerald slips out of bed very, very carefully, pausing every few seconds in her progress to evaluate Forest's comatose sleep. She throws a blue silk kimono around her shoulders, and at her dresser, she draws a manila folder from the top drawer. With one last glance at her beloved husband, she carries the folder down the stairs to the dining table. At her computer, she deletes everything she has written.

She carries a handful of blank paper to her table and writes, muttering an occasional word aloud, and then adds words to the sentence with pen. She writes in script. Japanese. She stops writing thirty minutes later. She reads the six new pages she has written in kanji, inserts them between the folder's cover, closes the folder and moves it aside so that when she lowers her head into her arms her tears will not stain the paper.

At four-forty-five, she returns to her bedroom and, in the darkness, slips the folder into the top drawer of her dresser. Standing at the window as she removes her robe, she glances outside. A streetlight sends a filtered mix of glow and shadow through the rain to the cars parked along both curbs of the wet street.

Her hands fly to her face when she notices the front bumper of a sleek white Thunderbird close against the rear bumper of Forest's red Toyota. She squints and stares until the face behind the windshield, inside the windshield, becomes clear, identifiable.

Anthony Coniglio.

After draping her robe around her shoulders, she goes down the dark stairs again, this time not to the dining room but to the kitchen. She moves to the counter, and the redwood rack that contains her meticulously selected collection of knives for the slicing or chopping of beef or chicken or vegetables. She draws three free, evaluates each. The choice is a long, narrow, and very sharp blade for boning beef or poultry.

Returning the other two knives to their slots Emerald leaves the kitchen, the long knife at her side, its needle tip brushing the silk of her robe to the right of her kneecap.

At the side of the bed, out of sight of the white Thunderbird, Emerald kneels to lay the knife on the rug beneath her meticulously folded silk robe. Then, sliding beneath the blankets, she shapes her body to Forest's. Flesh against flesh, she lies there, her wet cheek pressed into the warm robe tightened across his beloved shoulder. Her fingers seek their way in between the fingers of his right hand, moving delicately so she will not awaken him.

༺༒༻

At five-thirty, when the doorbell shatters Forest's sleep, he pulls his hand free of Emerald's fingers, slowly tugs and pushes his body out of the bed so he will not disturb his beloved's sleep. He stumbles downstairs, barely conscious enough to wonder who might be demanding attention at such an hour. Western Union? A telegram? Emerald's parents?

When he opens the door Tony Coniglio, leaning against the panel, falls inside, onto his knees. Forest clutches at Tony's sleeve to help him rise but, scratching at the frame, Tony succeeds in pulling himself erect. Tony is drunk. Very drunk.

"I come in, Forest?"

"Sure. Come in. Hey, you look rough. You might not know it, but someone poured a pint of blood in each of your eyes."

"I sit down?"

"Of course. But it's—Jesus Christ, it's not even six o'clock. In the *morning*. What the hell are you doing driving Berkeley streets at six in the morning? And you're looped. I've never seen you drunk before. I'll make us some coffee and wake Emerald."

"She's awake. She was at the bedroom window just now."

"You saw her at the window? Christ! Well, she's not herself lately. Last night I couldn't sleep, and she slept like a rock. So she might at least be resting. I'll go get her."

"Wait a minute, man. I have to talk to you. Alone."

"What about? Can it wait till I get the coffee on?"

"You know, man, sometimes this job's the shits." Tony, on one of the six oak chairs that circle the kitchen table, stretches out his legs and closes his eyes. "I try to be fair, I try to stay right on the center line. I work hard to be compassionate, but the law's the law and I believe in the law, man. I'd bust my own mother if she—"

"You said that the other night. What's this all about, Tony?"

215

Tony takes a deep breath, shakes his head as if trying to clear it of pain, and then he lets the stored words tumble out. He has probably been sitting in his car for hours preparing for this moment.

"Emerald. She was with Farleigh O'Brien the morning he died. She drove over—"

"Wait a minute."

"You better sit down, man, or this will put you down."

Forest waits, trying to comprehend the words Tony has served him. Bits of food he probably won't want to taste or, if tasted, not want to swallow.

"You were in Missouri. I have a witness who confirms that Emerald left this house at five o'clock that morning. A neighbor. I have two witnesses—one of them O'Brien's landlady—who confirm that Emerald stayed with Farleigh for three hours that morning. The coroner verifies O'Brien's being shot before eight. Around seven or seven-thirty, probably.

"Emerald was at the cafe on the first floor of her office building ten minutes after it opened, their first customer that morning. She ordered coffee to go and a muffin. When she left the cafe, she forgot the muffin. She was seated at her desk when Mr. Breitbach walked in at eight-fifteen. Mr. Breitbach has always been the first person to arrive at the office. This was the first time in ten years Emerald was there before him."

Since when is forgetting, not eating, a muffin a felony?

"I got permission yesterday to put a tap on your phone. That's how I know Emerald called Kyoto last night. She talked to her parents. For an hour. An hour and six minutes, to be exact. You can see a translation of their conversation.

"Emerald told her parents maybe twenty times that she loved them, that she should never have left Kyoto. She raved about how much she loved you—twenty

216

times maybe—but you were too good for her. Too good, too noble. She does not deserve you. You deserve better."

Emerald. Kyoto. Her parents. Emerald must have been more worried about her mother and father than she'd appeared to be. Why hadn't she mentioned their conversation? She knew he was worried about them, too. He didn't have to start teaching for five months. They will fly to Japan immediately. He will finally meet the Hyashis. Emerald will be giddy, showing him the scenes she has described so many times in such detail with such delight.

"Emerald killed Farleigh O'Brien, Forest. Maria Scarborough's involved. She's talked to us. Admitted everything. Forest, they've both been carrying on with O'Brien. Maria for a year, Emerald for five months. We got the witnesses, confession, lab work. We found hairs.

"After we had other evidence that indicated Emerald's involvement I collected some hair samples here the other night. Lab work confirmed everything. It's all there. I'll be getting an indictment out today. Media will have it in about an hour. That's as long as I can hold them off."

Tony holds his head in his hands, sobs for a minute, produces a handkerchief, blows his nose.

"It's all there, man. I wanted you to know before—yeah, sit down, man. You want me to get you something? Water? How about that coffee? I can make coffee."

Forest, for whatever reason, feels and sees himself standing on the top of a boxcar speeding down a railroad track. Looming ahead, hurtling toward him—a bridge. If he doesn't drop, he'll surely be beheaded. The name *Emerald* repeats in his ears, inside his head, like waves pounding a beach where he lies in the sand dreaming of...

Of what? Of love? Of peace? Of Emerald?

The train speeds on, his head slices through the bridge as if the steel is mush.

Tony, standing before him, holds out a steaming cup of coffee. Where has that come from? Who made it? Has Emerald finally come downstairs?

Emerald...Emerald...

He has to go upstairs to wake Emerald, to tell her Tony is here, but when he tries to stand his knees turn gelid and he falls back into the chair.

"Shall I go get Emerald, Forest?"

Tony's voice is solicitous, the voice of a son appealing to his ailing father to please get well. Forest gropes for a fragment of hope. Tony has changed his mind, Tony wants to admit he's mistaken. He has found someone else, he just had a phone call...while he was making the coffee...informing him of the true identity of the killer. Maria. That's who it was. Maria killed Farleigh O'Brien. Jesus, he has to call Paul. Paul will need him now more than ever.

"You're wrong, Tony."

Forest turns his head, sees, on the counter of the antique cabinet across the room, photographs taken fifteen years ago, twelve years ago, five years ago, two months ago. Emerald in every one—laughing, looking into his camera, laughing into his heart. Nine representations of Emerald's face to the world. Laughing.

They've both been carrying on with O'Brien, Forest...They've both been...

Maria and Emerald have been sleeping with O'Brien.

Fact. It is a fact. As factual as Tony's presence in this house at this moment.

Forest has always suspected that swooning is reserved for nineteenth century maidens—for Bronte, for Austen—but here he is, swooning.

He hears...sees...Tony Coniglio leave the room. Five minutes later, ten minutes, half an hour later, a day later, Tony is standing before him. He looks sick, as if he's about to collapse.

"I'm okay now," Forest says. He gets to his feet, balances himself, remains standing. "I'll go get Emerald," he says. He will hold her in his arms forever, will love her forever, will forgive her forever. They will spend every penny they have on the best lawyers, the best doctors.

He starts for the stairs, but Tony grabs him.

"No, man. No. You can't go up there. You don't want to go up there."

He struggles, but Tony's arms bind him so tightly he has difficulty breathing.

"Emerald's dead, Forest. Emerald's sitting on a mat in the bathroom. She's stabbed herself. Emerald's *dead*, Forest. Stop, you can't go up there, man. I won't let you go up there."

Tony tosses him back onto the chair.

"I've called the ambulance. In five minutes, there's gonna be a dozen technicians and medical people in here. Probably radio and TV, too."

He takes several paces back, still prepared to stop Forest should he try a rush for the stairs.

"Oh, man, what I'd give to change all this. Oh, man...please, Forest...that's it. Relax. Relax. Aw, shit, man..."

⤙⤚

Neither Paul nor Maria attend the funeral—Maria, because she is being held by the San Francisco police, Paul because he has disappeared. Forest has a Japanese friend of Emerald's call her parents in Kyoto, and though they both want to come they agree that Emerald's mother cannot endure the rigors of the trip and, especially, the ceremony. Her father decides to stay in Kyoto to care for his wife.

Several colleagues from Saint Catherine's are present at the funeral, including the president and eight or nine other Brothers. And Jeanne. She embraces Forest, her face dark, wet.

The English department has sent banks of flowers, and just about every instructor has come, several of them having had to cancel their classes. After the ceremony, the president assures Forest he, as well as Professor Scarborough, should take off as much time as they need. A semester. Two semesters. The college will cover their salaries. The president is trying to communicate with Professor Scarborough, but no one knows his whereabouts. The two Scarborough children, both of whom are present, come forward to embrace Forest.

Perhaps, Brother President suggests, perhaps Forest knows the whereabouts of Professor Scarborough?

Forest shakes his head, tries and fails to say no. The president stands on tiptoe and reaches up to put an arm around Forest's shoulders.

"You take as much time as you need," he says.

<hr />

During the following weeks Forest sits in the house and tries to comprehend his loss. Twice he awakes in the middle of the night with chest pains, torn between the fear of death and the yearning for it. When he reaches across the pillow to find nothing, no one, he calls out, "Emerald." She must be in the bathroom. Or downstairs. He knows she used the dining room table for her writing. She is still writing that book.

When he finds the folder in the drawer of her desk—he has to pry it open with a screwdriver, chipping the edge but not caring about its now depreciated value. He leafs through the pages, hoping for drawings, for a few words in English; but her ideas, her comments, her reasons for writing, are in very elaborate Japanese script. Emerald wanted her work to be a secret, so a secret it will remain. He burns every page, one at a time, and then the folder as well.

⤳

The first week after the funeral, one or another member of the English department, even the new instructors who hadn't met Emerald or barely know Forest, stay with him each night. They try to play chess with him, try to include him in viewing performances on public television, try to get him out of the house to cafes or to their own homes. He sits, shaking his head, staring at what might be called space were it not a solid wall. True space, beyond the wall, is, after all, where Emerald now dwells. As once she had dwelled in this house, in his bed, in his arms.

Jeanne visits him two days after the funeral. He starts to apologize for not having known that Mary Beth had actually died. In truth, he has not even thought about Mary Beth until this moment. Jeanne understands. Mary Beth, she says, had been cremated, as she had requested. The entire English department had attended the ceremonies.

"I guess," Jeanne says, "the English department is just about funeraled out."

When she prepares to leave, she takes Forest into her arms and thanks him for his kindnesses to Mary Beth.

"If you want to stay with me for a while, I'd like it," she says. "Or I can come here. Maybe we can help each other. Let me know."

"You're stronger than I am, Jeanne. I think I have to be alone for a while."

Jeanne nods, descends the steps then returns.

"I decided you ought to know," she says. "I knew Mary Beth well enough to know she'd not be angry."

"Angry?"

221

"Why Mary Beth had to give the impression that she wasn't gay I don't know, but Forest, she never slept with Farleigh O'Brien. She told me that. I believe her. She never lied to me. Maybe she felt you and the others—well, I'm no psychologist, but I know she's been gay, completely gay, since high school.

"You might say it doesn't matter now. It does to me. I don't want lies or insinuations hanging around my memory of her. I loved Mary Beth. She loved me. They say that's all that matters. Anyway, if you need company and want to stay with me for a while, call me."

Standing there in the rain, she gives Forest the most endearing smile she has probably ever offered any human except Mary Beth Lederberg.

Why should he feel ashamed? Depleted? Why should he be trying to frame an apology? Here he is, at the advanced age of fifty-six, about to ponder his needs, his motives, his emotions, about to consider decisions he should have considered twenty, thirty years before. Here he is, a moderately reputable teacher who has given his life to the preparation of his mind for the analysis of feelings, ideas, language; and here is a simple, trusting woman of limited education humbling him with her faith in something so mundane as lost love.

In wondering about Jeanne's natural ability to survive, he turns quite reasonably to his own ability. Call it willingness. Does he care to survive without some sense, some knowledge of the reasons he had submitted so willingly to Paul Scarborough's depravities—yes, that is the appropriate term, depravities—for thirty years? Had some colleague given himself to a bizarre and destructive religion, tithing all his possessions, mental and physical, to his leader, he, Forest, would have vilified the supplicant as a self-destructive psychotic. But Paul had led and Forest had followed without resistance, without question. Forest, the will-

222

ing slave, had offered himself to the tyrant for slaughter. Sick. Sick sick sick.

Maria's lawyer calls to inform him that Maria wants very much to talk to him. After the trial date has been set, she will be released on her own recognizance, at high bail. Her daughter is coming to Berkeley to live with her. Maria told the lawyer to ask Forest if he wants to stay with them when she returns home.

Forest drives his Toyota for the first time since the funeral. Emerald had loved these hillside roads. As the car points its red nose up into the forest of eucalyptus trees, he hears her laughter in the wind, bounding out of the many hidden paths they had hiked. The memories join the hard rain and the greasy windshield wipers to blind him, distract him. He makes several wrong turns, and has difficulty locating the Scarborough's house, which had been a second home to him for so many years.

Eventually, he makes the correct turn onto Tamalpais Road. Maria is very thin. Her eyes seem to have been sucked back inside her head. Her hair has been cut so short she is almost bald.

"So I wouldn't look too attractive, I guess," she says, when Forest stares at what had once been a tumble of blond curls.

He follows her into the living room and takes a chair before the fire. Nina, Maria's daughter, says, "Hello, Forest, I'm glad you're here. Can I get you some coffee? I made an apple pie."

"Just coffee. Black would be fine, Nina. Thanks."

"Mum?"

"Tea, darling."

Then they sit, each of them stymied. How begin the conversation? How even look at each other? How, why, pretend to be rational?

"Nina's sweats," Maria says, pulling the belt of the pants away from her waist. "Twice too big."

"You've lost weight."

223

"Twenty pounds. Do you want to talk, Forest?"

"I don't think I can, Maria."

"I have to tell you a few things. I must. You don't have to talk. If you want me to stop, say so."

He does not want her to start, but he does not protest when she begins, nor does he depart, though his hands cling to the familiar knobs of the armrest as if he is preparing to bolt from the chair and rush away from this house.

"Neither Emerald nor I knew the other had been sleeping with him, Forest. We found out when Farleigh told me he had HIV, he was sick, was getting sicker, was possibly dying. I took an exam. Negative. Doctor said I could show positive later if I'd been infected. It could be incubating.

"I was terrified. And furious. I told Emerald about me and Farleigh. It was then she told me she'd been sleeping with him, too. She took an exam. Negative. Doctor told her she could test positive next time or the time after, or several years later, if she was infected. That's the way the disease works."

"Emerald thought she had AIDS, you thought you had AIDS, you both believed Farleigh O'Brien had AIDS because he told you he did. Is that right?"

"That's right."

"It's possible he didn't have AIDS, it's possible neither you nor Emerald had AIDS."

"That's right."

"Why would Farleigh...?"

"I don't know. I can't even guess. He was a worthless bastard. I know that. I know something else, Forest."

Forest waits.

"Emerald loved you, Forest. In my own way, I loved Paul. Why'd I go to Farleigh? Because Paul hated him, I guess. Who knows? I can't even remember which came first. I'd given up on Freud and Jung and Adler and Horney before I left college, so I don't spend much time trying to assess blame. Or guilt.

"After Farleigh told me he was dying of AIDS, after I had my checkup, I couldn't, wouldn't, let Paul in me. I'd not infect him, I'd not let him be punished for my crime. Crime's not the right word, perhaps. But I was determined to protect him. I discovered Emerald felt the same. About you."

As Maria continues to talk, he has tried to connect her story with Emerald's behavior over the last several months. There is a connection, but what is it? Punished for my crime...punished for her crime...Emerald's crime? Maria's crime? Farleigh's crime? No, he just cannot complete the puzzle.

"An hour after Farleigh told me he had AIDS, I bought a gun. We were going to go over together, Emerald and me. Emerald insisted she do it alone. She talked about the ancient Samurai code. She had to honor that code. I have no code. I never did. But it was me who thought it all out. I planned it all. I was the expert. Please don't hate me, for God's sake, don't hate me."

Hate?

"But how dare I request that of you?"

When he looks at her, he is thinking, I've had more perfect years with Emerald than any man could hope to have in a long lifetime. How could I hate anyone?

He says, "I don't hate you, Maria. But why would Emerald...?"

No words exist for that question to complete itself.

Maria shrugs. "I don't know. She'd spent hours with him translating, writing, discussing Zen. He was more than her guru. He was...maybe he was her American Mishima. Who knows? I don't. Do you?"

Why hadn't she told him? Why hadn't he known? And—this with great anguish—why had she

225

never been moved to discuss her interest in Zen with him, her Forest, her husband, her more-than-guru?

"He charmed her. The way he'd charmed me, the way he'd charmed that Mexican girl. The one he knocked up. The way he charmed his students, the way he charmed his—your—colleagues. The way he charmed his admiring audiences. The way he charmed every living soul he ever met. Except you and Paul."

"Why...why, Emerald?"

"I don't know, Forest. I know Emerald loved you. But once it happened she was, well, ashamed. That's all. Dirty and ashamed beyond redemption. I tried to convince her she could go back, she could forget. She just shook her head and said over and over how evil she was, how godly you were. She was dead, really, before she died, when she realized what she'd done to you."

Nina, entering the room—has she been listening from the kitchen?—is trembling so badly and sniffling so hard she loses control of the tray, which tilts, sending cups and saucers to the tiled floor in front of the fireplace. A stew of shards and coffee and cream and sugar flow across the hearth. She kneels on the tiles, her legs and feet in the mess, her sandals soaked, steaming. Her back to Forest and her mother, she covers her face with her palms and weeps.

"I'm afraid for Paul," Maria says, as if the mess on the floor and Nina's tears are a natural part of a guest's entertainment. "He's not as resilient as you are. Not as—well, not as forgiving." She presses down and kisses the top of Nina's curls. "It's okay, darling, it's okay. I'll clean it up. Forget it."

Nina shakes her head and leaves the room.

"He'll blame himself. That's the worst thing I have to live with. Paul thought, when I stopped screwing him, that I no longer loved him. Maybe I

226

didn't. Maybe love leaped out our windows a long time ago."

When Forest leaves the house, he reassures Nina, holding her, saying he knows he doesn't have to ask her to take care of her mother. He is tempted, purely for the sake of protocol, for Nina's sake, perhaps, to say that should they hear from Paul they should call him, but he cannot get the words out.

⤛

A night alone for once.

He erases all material from the computer related to *Murder by Metaphor*. He spends several hours burning papers—old letters, notes for courses taught over the years at Saint Catherine's, bills, research data and early and recent drafts of pages for the Twain article.

Here is the envelope of Mary Beth's that Jeanne had pressed into his hand the night Mary Beth was taken to the hospital. Hundreds of pages in three separate brown folders, all three enclosed in one larger red folder. Everything indexed. Her completed articles, ideas for as-yet unwritten articles, letters to, letters from, bits and pieces of conversation noted, clippings, pages of scribblings destined apparently for a journal. A white index card clipped to the front of the red folder.

> Forest: Much of my recent academic life enclosed here. Do with it what you will. I'll say goodbye now. One important caveat: forget what I've said about Max Goldstein, forget what he's said about me, forget, in fact, most of what he might have said about himself. Poor naive man, he fell in love with me and I had to hurt him to help him save himself. Max lives in a weirder, denser fantasy

world than I do. Farleigh? I never understood the man. Now I never will. Will anyone? Hope the rest of your and Emerald's lives remain peaceful, Forest.—M.B.L.

Forest stuffs the folders and papers inside the manila envelope, along with the note, and lays it all on top of the burning wood. He wants nothing to remind him of anything in this house, this college, this town.

≈

Midnight. The house dark and creaking in the wind. "Risten," Emerald used to say, "God cracking knuckohs."

He leaves the bed and goes downstairs to his study. He has not bothered to slip on his robe, so now, shivering a bit, he stuffs more papers into the fireplace on top of the thick body of ashes and puts a match to them. He adds a few sticks of kindling and observes the progress of the fire until the flames catch the wood.

Nothing to remind him of anything.

But he does want something. *Citizen Kane.* He's seen the film twenty times at least and fell in love with Dorothy Commingore, the actress who played the magnate's mistress. *Rosebud!* The word visible on the sled as it is devoured by the flames. Why is he in the study? What is he looking for?

All about him are stacks of books tied with cord. People from the public library will be coming shortly after breakfast to pick them up. Hundreds of books. Perhaps thousands. The collection of his lifetime. He does not want them. He wants nothing.

But he must be wanting something. Why else is he kneeling on the floor, turning the lamp to focus on this stack, that stack, this stack? What is he looking for?

"No poetry anywhere," he says, only partly aware that he has spoken the words aloud. He is shivering quite seriously now. How long has he been sitting here in this cold room? Gray dawn shows in the eastern window.

"God crimbs up out of sea now," Emerald said. "He shakes hair dry. Sunbeams."

Emerald is dust. That thick black hair, that creamy skin, and, oh, the huge black eyes—all dust.

He stumbles up the steps, crawls into bed and is immediately warm. He will sleep for hours. For days. The library? He'll hear the bell, he'll go down to the front door, he'll let them take the books.

He dreams. His mother, in the kitchen, pours hot water from the pot into her mug of powdered coffee. She says something about poets or poetry. In his dream he cries out, "Momma!"

December 17, 1993

Dear Brother President:

It has been a difficult time for me. I'm not prepared to teach again. Please consider this letter my resignation from the college. I'd come on campus whenever Personnel has the forms for me, whatever they are, but I'd prefer they be mailed to me. Is that possible?

I want to thank you and everyone else at the college, especially my colleagues in the English Department, for all your kindnesses. I was not prepared for that. Nor can I sleep easily recalling my private fantasies that judged so much at Saint Cate's as evil.

I cannot speak for Professor Scarborough, but I for one am apologizing here for all the pains and frustrations I've caused you personally over the years. My despairs were of my own making, not yours. I have a buyer for my home and so will be moving somewhere outside of California, where I can cope with my nightmares in a place that has no ghosts. My thanks to you, Brother.....

Sincerely...
Forest Butler,
Professor
English Department

December 22, 1993

Dear Brother...

As you can imagine, it's been a difficult time for me. I have decided that I cannot live in this house or this city any longer. For that reason please consider this letter a formal decision to resign from the faculty. I can't suitably express my appreciation for all your kindnesses and those of my colleagues, especially those in the English Department. I intend to sell my home and move somewhere, perhaps New England. Or perhaps New Mexico, a state Emerald had always hoped to visit. Should it be possible for the Personnel Office to mail me the necessary forms for both my res-

ignation and my retirement funds,
could you please inform them to do
so? I'd prefer not to come on campus.
Again, Brother, my gratitude.

Forest writes five letters to the president but decides
to send the second one.

January 6, 1994

Dear Maria...

I've sold the house and will be
leaving town next Monday. Your at-
torney informed me that I might be
called to testify. I'll send you my address and phone number.

Remember, Paul fought in the
Korean War, he was in and out of
hospitals. He's a survivor. I hope
things turn out well for you, Maria.

Forest

January 6, 1994

Dear Bonnie:

Thanks for your note. I guess now
our exchanges of condolences have
come to an end. I'll be leaving
Berkeley tomorrow. To where, I don't
yet know.

You've heard, you tell me, that
I'm doing a book about Farleigh. I'm
not. I'm giving my computer away. I
quit Saint Catherine's. From here on
I'll be watching films on my VCR,
reading fiction (everybody's writing it)
and trying not to sleep.

I'll send you an address and telephone number when I settle in

somewhere. Should you not respond I'll understand.

Can we endure whatever's left of our lives? I hope so, Bonnie.

Sincere best wishes...
Forest

Taos, New Mexico
February 20, 1994

Dear Bonnie...

When I sold my house and got rid of all my books I found this copy of a poem Farleigh wrote...it's a letter/poem to seven-year-old Dylanna. The only memento I did not burn.

I don't think he ever published the poem. I don't know why. It's as good, I think, as anything he wrote. Tender, sentimental but honest. I thought Dylanna might like to have it. My best to you and her. And, believe it or not, if he were alive, I'd wish the best to Farleigh, too.

Your 7th Birthday

At the party when you laughed
monarch butterflies hovered
in the lavender.
You were disappointed when
I gave you your gift. Forgive me.
I'll do better.
I did not remember
what it means to be seven.
Next year you'll be eight.
Will I not remember again?
When you're 45, as I am now,

I'll be 83.
Surely I'll remember then
when I will be 83.
Will I be 83? Will I be?

❧

"Hey, man, how you doin'?"

"Okay. As well as can be expected. How the hell did you know I'm in Wellfleet?"

"Hey, I'm a detective. Anyway, I'm here. I have some late reports. Interested?"

"Not especially."

"Can I take you to lunch?"

"No, thanks, Tony."

"I've done enough damage. Right? Okay." He embraces Forest and starts to leave. "Call me, man. Anytime. Whatever you need, call me. Would you do that?"

"Sure."

Tony reaches the door and is about to walk out into the hot summer air.

"Tell me," Forest says.

Tony does not turn to face him but speaks into the screen door. "Autopsy on O'Brien showed no HIV infection. Nothing. Niente. Nada. Paul Scarborough never served in Korea. He was a conscientious objector. Papers, medals, all counterfeit. Maria Scarborough knew that, way back. Have you been reading the papers or watching TV?"

"No."

"Maria got five years. She'll probably serve eighteen months. Maybe less."

When Forest walks Tony onto the porch he sees the rented car in the driveway.

"You gonna settle in here, Forest? New England ain't California, man."

"I don't know, Tony."

233

"I'll keep in touch, man. You're gonna see a lot of me over the years. No matter where you hide. God love you, man."

END

ABOUT THE AUTHOR

Born in Pennsylvania coal-mine town of North Butler in 1923, CHESTER AARON was an amateur boxer in high school and fought in the Golden Gloves. A machine-gunner with the 70th Armored Infantry Battalion in WWII, he participated in the liberation of Dachau. After graduating from UC Berkeley, he worked first as an x-ray technician, then was a professor for 25 years at Saint Mary's College in California. A garlic farmer and internationally known expert on the subject, he grows more than eighty varieties from thirty countries. As an author, he has published eighteen works in both fiction and nonfiction, adult and young-adult. One book became a movie; two books have been optioned recently for film.

ABOUT THE ARTIST

GARY TROW has worked as an artist since graduating in 2003 with a First Class honors BA in Illustration from the Arts Institute at Bournemouth.

He began by working part-time at magazines before moving on to 3-D visualization and computer games. Now, he's finally producing book covers, the reason he went back to university as a mature student, ("Well, I say mature...") and is also working towards putting together his first exhibition of paintings. Please feel free to visit and comment at http://gary.trow.artistportfolio.net.

LaVergne, TN USA
07 October 2009
160116LV00001B/7/P